WHO'S THE JUNIOR HIGH HUNK?

JUNIOR HIGH

Junior High Jitters
Class Crush
The Day the Eighth Grade Ran the School
How Dumb Can You Get?
Eighth Grade to the Rescue
Eighth Grade Hero?
Those Crazy Class Pictures
Starring the Eighth Grade
Who's the Junior High Hunk?

WHO'S THE JUNIOR HIGH HUNK?

Kate Kenyon

SCHOLASTIC INC.
New York Toronto London Auckland Sydney

ISBN 0-590-41388-0

12 11 10 9 8 7 6 5 4 3 2 3 4 5 6/9

Printed in the U.S.A. 01

First Scholastic printing, March 1988

Chapter 1

As the girl sailed down the center aisle, every boy in Mr. Armand's French class sat up taller. Every girl tried not to stare. And Mr. Armand stopped conjugating the verb *vivre* right in the middle of a sentence.

The girl wore a flowing challis wrap skirt and a rose-colored body suit that exactly matched the delicate color of her high cheekbones. The color was the perfect complement to her thick and glossy shoulder-length black hair.

"Oh, good, Monique, you're here!" Mr. Armand said. "Class, I'd like you to meet Monique Gorgée from France. She's a new foreign exchange student over at the high school. And she has graciously offered to do without study hall for a few weeks so that the eighth grade will have the chance to converse with a native French speaker."

Reaching the front of the room, Monique

turned to face the class, her skirt and hair swirling artfully around her. She perched gracefully on the front edge of Mr. Armand's desk. Lifting her hand, she gave the class a distinctive wave, a charming little salute, and a wink of one mascaraed sea-green eye. The silver bracelets she wore, which were covered with tiny bells, fell to her elbow making pleasant, tinkly sounds.

"*Bonjour!*" she said. "I am called Moni for short. I am in the ninth grade, but some of you will see me in your biology and American history classes here at Cedar Grove's Junior High because in those I am — how you say? — *sotte* student! Ah, yes, stupid!"

Under cover of the class's appreciative laughter, Nora Ryan leaned across the aisle. "She has the figure, face, *and* grace to be a big-time model!" she said to Jennifer Mann. "Too bad she's a shrimp like me."

"Neither of you is a shrimp," whispered Jennifer, who was not only Nora's best friend but also her staunchest supporter. "You're both just — how you say? — *petite!*"

The two giggled behind their hands. "Gee, Jen, you're really turning into a French whiz," Nora said.

Jennifer went back to staring at Monique, as everybody was. But Nora glanced down at her own clothes — jeans and boots topped by an oversized sweater. Nora's older sister Sally called it her "oatmeal" sweater because it was off-white with flecks of brown wool the same color as Nora's short curly hair. When Nora had studied herself in the mirror that morning, she'd felt casually stylish, together. Now, comparing herself to the French newcomer, she decided she looked about as exciting as oatmeal.

Jennifer was fingering a lock of her own hair, which seemed to be almost identical to Moni's in color and texture. Would her hair bounce and swirl like Monique's if she cut it to shoulder length like that? Jen wondered. She made a mental note to get Nora's opinion later.

Meanwhile, wearing big grins, Mr. Armand and Monique were conversing with each other in rapid-fire French.

Whispers flew around the room: "What are they talking about?" "What are they saying?"

Good-looking Tommy Ryder, three seats behind Jennifer, opened his mouth to say "It's Greek to me!" but stopped himself just in time.

"Too corny and dumb, Ryder," he muttered to himself. Moni was smooth and sophisticated — so he'd better act that way, too, if he wanted to get her interested in him.

"They *all* fall for you sooner or later," he assured himself, "but it's better to be safe than sorry." He clamped a hand over his mouth when he realized he'd been speaking aloud, then quickly glanced around to see if anyone had heard. Unfortunately, his buddy, Mitch Pauley, seated across the aisle, was grinning at him.

"Too corny and dumb, Ryder," Mitch whispered, stifling a bellow of laughter.

Tommy pretended not to hear.

At Mr. Armand's request, Monique was going around the room asking each person a question in French. "Give your answer *en Français*," Mr. Armand ordered the class.

"What do you like to eat for dinner?" Moni asked Jennifer.

The class roared with laughter when Jennifer — one of whose many causes was working against cruelty to animals — accidentally replied "Baked cat."

But instead of joining the laughter, Moni gave Jennifer a sympathetic little half-smile. "That is not so bad a mistake," she said. "Once, in London, I spent a whole hour walking up and down a busy street asking people where I could find a bottle. What I meant to say was bathroom! They all must have thought I was a crazee —

how you say? — a crazee . . . crazee . . . bag lady!" She threw back her head with a husky but merry laugh, in which the class eagerly joined.

Moni was not only adorable, she was nice and sympathetic, too, Nora thought.

The bell rang, and several of the boys in the class rushed toward Monique. Mitch, with the combination of long legs and speed that had made him captain of nearly every sports team at Cedar Groves Junior High, reached her first.

But it was Tommy who had the smoothest line: "Am I glad you're here, Monique Gorgée! I desperately need a private tutor due to the fact that I am such a *sotte* student in French."

Moni's husky, melodious laugh rang out. "Only girls can be *sotte* students!" she said. "You, a boy, are just plain *sot*!"

Tommy turned the color of watermelon, but he and the rest of the besotted boys trailed after Moni as she swept out the door.

Back inside the classroom, Nora and Jennifer were doubled over with laughter.

"That," managed Nora, "was just about the classiest insult I've ever heard!"

Chapter 2

Later that afternoon, Jen banged her locker door closed and whirled around, holding a big handful of her hair up so that what showed was only shoulder-length. "What do you think, Nora?" she shouted over the jubilant after-school noise in the school's main corridor. "Would my hair look as good as Moni's at this length?"

Nora turned from her own locker. She cocked her head first to the right, then to the left, squinting thoughtfully at Jennifer. "Moni has more natural curl than you do, Jen. I think that's what makes her hair so swingy. I'm afraid if you cut yours it might just . . . just . . . "

"Hang there?" Jennifer supplied.

Nora laughed, embarrassed. As frequently happened, Jennifer seemed to read her mind, just as she often felt she could read Jen's. "Hey, listen, you don't want to cut your hair anyway," Nora said quickly.

"You've had it that long practically since the day I met you. I mean, remember that time Steve Crowley decided to give you rainbow hair with his finger paints? Remember how Mrs. Gillingham washed your hair four times and it still came out sort of murky?"

"Oh, pul-leez. Please spare us another best-friend-since-kindergarten story, Nora," sniped Susan Hillard, who had joined the girls, along with Tracy Douglas.

Tracy widened her big blue eyes. "You've been writing stories, Nora?" she asked.

Susan slapped her forehead in exasperation. "I'm talking about the ones she and Jen *tell*, Swifty. The ones we've heard eight million times."

"Eight million and one," Nora said, exchanging a grin with Jennifer.

"Well, just don't start boring poor Monique Gorgée to death with those old stories," Susan said. "I mean, they just make us all sound so . . . so . . . middle class!"

"Isn't Moni absolutely adorable?" Tracy cried, twirling the lock on her locker. She moved over a little so that Lucy Armanson, who had just arrived, could get to her own locker. "Today, for the first time in my life, I actually wished I was a brunette instead of a blonde," Tracy continued. She opened her locker and peered critically at her shiny blonde hair in the mirror she had glued inside the door.

"Are you guys talking about the new foreign exchange student?" Lucy asked, throwing a gray suede blazer over the purple silk blouse she was wearing. "If so, I, as usual, have the official scoop." Her eyes twinkled, and she patted her short Afro with mock smugness.

Nora laughed. "One of these days, guys, she's going to start charging us for the juicy stuff she overhears while working in the administration office."

It was Lucy's turn to laugh. "I didn't have to overhear it this time. Monique *told* me. I talked to her for a while when she was waiting to register for the two junior high classes she'll be taking."

"Biology and American history," the four other girls said, practically in unison.

Lucy was disappointed that they already had at least some information about the new girl. "Well, I bet you don't know that she's fourteen and from Fleur, one of the most exclusive suburbs of Paris. Her father owns an international chain of French bakeries, so she's traveled a lot. She's spent months in cities like Los Angeles, New York, and London."

"Sounds like she has a lot in common with Denise," Jennifer said. "Maybe she even went to a Swiss boarding school, like Denise did."

"Wow, the future heiress of an international cosmetics company and the future heiress of an international chain of French bakeries right here in little old Cedar Groves," Nora drawled.

"Well, I bet Moni is even more up on what's hot in fashion than Denise is," said Lucy, who always looked like she'd stepped out of the fashion pages of a magazine herself. "I mean, Paris is the fashion capital of the world. And Denise may have lived there at one time, but she wasn't *born* there, like Monique was. And she doesn't know anyone there now."

Just then, Moni herself came around the corner and approached the group. "*Pardon*! But I am lost. How do I find the teacher lounge? I must speak to Mr. Armand."

Nora gave her directions, then racked her brain for something else to say to Moni, something that would make the French girl want to stay and talk for a while.

Tracy and Lucy obviously had the same idea.

"Where did you get those beautiful bracelets?" Tracy asked.

"What do you call those great-looking bracelets?" Lucy asked at exactly the same time.

"In Paris, these are all the rage right now," Moni said, holding up her arm so that the bracelets fell, tinkling, to her elbows. "We just call them our *clochettes*. Our bells, I mean." She took one off and handed it to Tracy to examine.

"I love that shade," Lucy said, gesturing at Moni's body suit. "So bright colors are back in style? Is that what's happening with the French designers?"

"Oh, yes, yes, yes, yes!" Moni exclaimed. "That gloom-and-doom all black-black-black Hollywood trash look is *fini*."

Jennifer saw that Nora, as well as the other girls, looked truly impressed by such internationally flavored sophistication. Tracy handed Jennifer Moni's bracelet, and Jennifer bent her head for a closer look at the tiny silver bells.

"Black," Moni continued, "may still be popular in one or two American and French — how you say? — oh, yes, hick towns! But in Paris and New York and L.A. it is very, very, very . . . oh, how you say, *passé*?"

Jennifer looked up from the bracelet to see that Moni had taken a small French/English dictionary from her pouchy shoulder bag. She was thumbing through it, unaware that a very, very, *very* annoyed Denise Hendrix — wearing black leather pants and a black leather motorcycle-style jacket — had joined the group and was standing behind Monique.

"We say *passé*, passé," Jennifer said quickly, in hopes that Moni would drop the subject. "It's a French word, but it's kind of gotten into our language, too."

But Moni didn't seem to hear her. "Passé," she read from the dictionary. "Past, bygone, faded, worn, withered."

Nora, Susan, Tracy, and Lucy laughed nervously as they, too, finally noticed Denise. Moni whirled around to see what they were looking at. Her cheeks turned scarlet as she took in Denise in her all-black outfit.

Nora took a deep breath. "Monique Gorgée, this is — "

"Denise Withered," Denise interrupted sarcastically, smiling coldly as she tossed a lock of shimmering blonde hair over her shoulder.

There was an awkward silence.

"You are so big!" Moni finally said to Denise, pronouncing it "beeg."

"Some people!" Denise said huffily. She flounced away from the group toward her own locker.

Moni looked like she was about to cry. "Is it not a compliment to be big here? In my country, since everyone is so short, it is a real asset to be as big as Denise. She must be five foot seven inches big!"

Nora laughed. "Oh, you mean *tall*," she said. "And it's an asset to be tall in America, too. Believe me, I should know! But big isn't the same as tall. Here, when you say a person — especially a girl — is big, you mean fat."

"Just remember that *big* rhymes with *pig*," Tracy said helpfully.

"Tracy Wadsworth Longfellow," Susan snickered.

"Don't worry about it, Moni," Jennifer said, her green eyes warm with sympathy. "Denise'll figure out what you meant, and she won't hold a grudge. After all, she knows what it's like to be in a place where you aren't one hundred percent fluent in the language."

Moni's eyes widened. "She does?"

"Yeah. Her family owns Denise Cosmetics," Tracy said. "They've traveled and lived all over the world."

"Including Paris," Nora said to Monique, handing her the bracelet.

To Nora's surprise, Moni gave her distinctive little wave and abruptly left the group without another word.

Meanwhile, Denise, carefully applying lip gloss at her locker, had been watching the group via the mirror of her compact. She was feeling a little guilty about stomping away like that. Talk about overreacting! She knew the French girl had been trying to comment on her height, not her weight. And as for Monique's cracks about black being out — Denise made a mental note to check out her mother's latest French *Vogue* — maybe she was even right about that. At any rate, the girl hadn't seen Denise when she'd made the remarks. She'd meant no harm. She was okay.

Then why, Denise asked herself, did she still feel so annoyed about the new girl? Why was it bugging her to see the other girls hang on to Monique's every word? To see them gushing over those bracelets and every other single item of clothing she was wearing?

"Because," Denise whispered aloud, forcing herself to look herself straight in the eye, "until today, that's how most of them behaved around *me*. Stop acting like an immature, jealous little kid, Denise!"

But she couldn't help suddenly feeling very sorry for herself. The girls were obviously and absolutely enchanted with the newcomer. So much so that not one of them had followed Denise to try to make her feel better. Not even Jennifer, whom Denise considered to be her closest friend in the bunch. There they were, probably consoling Moni, when it was *Denise* who had been insulted — even if it was an accidental insult!

She watched as Monique suddenly left

the group and the others girls finally — *finally* — headed for her.

"Moni has the type of figure that looks good in *any* kind of style," Tracy was saying as the group approached.

Lucy nodded. "Mm-hmm, she has an absolutely perfect figure."

Denise sighed with dismay and felt her temper rising. Wasn't this new fan club *ever* going to adjourn?

"She's too skinny," Denise snapped. "She has so little meat on her face that those high cheekbones make her look like a skeleton." Comically, she sucked in her cheeks to show the others what she meant.

Nora and Jennifer exchanged a look of surprise at Denise's outburst.

"I thought you said a person can't be too rich or too thin," Lucy said.

Denise felt like kicking herself for not remembering that. "I said *Gloria Vanderbilt* said that. I didn't."

Tracy pointed at the little swan insignia on the peach-colored designer sweatshirt she was wearing. "*This* Gloria Vanderbilt? The designer?"

Denise nodded.

"Well, *I* don't think Moni's too skinny," Nora said. "I think she's gorgeous. Even her name is gorgeous. Monique Gorgée."

Denise couldn't stop herself. "I hate to burst your bubble, but it sure isn't beautiful in French," she snapped. "*'Gorgée'* means 'gulp'!"

Jennifer glanced at Nora. This time Nora's eyes weren't wide with surprise. They were narrowed in anger.

"We haven't gotten that far in French yet," Jennifer said quickly, hoping to prevent an argument between her two friends.

"Well, it's from the verb *gorger*," Denise continued. "You know, to gorge one's self. To pig out."

Only Susan snickered at that remark.

"So her name translates as Monica Gulp," Denise went on. "That's about as foreign and exotic and gorgeous as Dorothy Gale from Kansas."

"Oh, did we get a new girl from Kansas, too?" Tracy asked.

"Dorothy Gale is in the *Wizard of Oz*," Susan said, hooting with laughter. "You're like the scarecrow from that movie, Tracy. Straw instead of brains."

Nora was really angry now. "She prefers to be called Moni, Denise. Moni Gorgée."

"Moni Gulp — even worse. No, make that *Boney* Gulp," Denise said, and then sucked in her cheeks again. "Boney Gulp — I love it!" she chortled over her shoulder as she waved good-bye and headed for the main door.

"That's terrible," Tracy said. "It sounds

like something *you* would come up with, Susan."

Susan looked offended. "I would not. I *like* Moni."

"Did anyone else just feel an earthquake?" Lucy asked.

Nora and Tracy shook their heads, puzzled.

Lucy laughed. "Well, Susan admitting that she actually *likes* someone is pretty earth-shaking stuff."

Jennifer wasn't paying any attention. She was watching Denise, who was leaving through the main door. "I wonder what's the matter with her?" Jen mumbled aloud.

Just then, Moni flew around the corner again and dodged into the center of the crowd, crouching down. "Hide me!" she pleaded. The girls crowded in protectively as Tommy, Mitch, and Steve Crowley came around the corner.

"Have you girls seen Moni Gorgeous?" Tommy asked.

"She ran that-a-away," Nora said, pointing down the hall. The boys headed off in that direction.

Moni emerged, wrinkling her nose. "Thank you. They are such *bébés*."

"You're telling *us*," Nora said.

Suddenly, Monique's eyes widened, and she stared down the corridor. Fifty yards away, a boy was practicing wheelies on his skateboard.

"Who is that?" Moni whispered. "He is so . . . so *attirant!*"

Nora stared at her, stunned. "Attractive?"

"No . . . um . . . oh, what is the word I want? He is such a . . . hunk! Hunk-hunk-hunk-HUNK! Oh, I must meet him!"

She ran off down the hall.

Tracy and Susan made the finger-down-throat gesture of disgust at each other. Lucy clutched her stomach and bent over, as if she were about to lose her lunch. Nora and Jen just stared at each other, mouths gaping.

Moni was hurrying toward *Jason Anthony!*

Chapter 3

Why Jason?

Jennifer put her pen down and stared at those words in her diary that evening. They were the last words of a paragraph she'd just written describing how Moni had made a run for him. Jennifer wrote the words again, this time adding capital letters and a couple of exclamation points:

WHY JASON?!!

She flopped over on her white chenille bedspread and stared at the ceiling, thinking. She and Nora had discussed Moni — and the Jason incident — all the way to Jennifer's house after school.

"Maybe she was so blinded by that red hair of his that she couldn't see how weird he was," Nora had said at one point.

Jen had laughed. "Well, just remember, we didn't get a chance to talk to her *after* she met him. She's probably seen the light by now. I mean, he probably picked his nose or something, just to gross her out."

By that time, they had reached the Manns' house and were going through the door to the kitchen.

"There will be no gross talk in here," Jeff, the Manns' housekeeper, had growled at them, though his blue eyes were twinkling. Jeff — who often made Jennifer think of a big graying teddy bear — was having a cup of coffee at the kitchen table with his girlfriend, Debby Kincaid. Jen loved him like a member of the family — because that was the way he acted, unlike the other housekeepers the Manns had endured before her dad had found Jeff. Jennifer's mother had died when she and her little brother Eric were very young.

Anyway, Jennifer wrote in her diary, *we sat down with Jeff and Debby and started to tell them all about Moni. But it turns out Debby has already met her. She says Moni is living with the Bryant family, just a couple of houses up the street from hers.*

Debby thinks Moni is absolutely adorable — just like we do — except for her strange reaction to Jason, of course!

The princess phone on Jennifer's night table rang and she reached for it, shouting "I'll get it!" She knew she really didn't have to bother shouting. Everyone in the Mann house knew Jen and Nora talked on the phone every night without fail at about this time.

"*Allô?*" Jen said cheerfully.

Nora groaned on the other end of the line. "Oh, Jen, no. You're not going to start copying Moni, are you? That's *so* seventh grade. Make that *sixth* grade. Wasn't that the year you walked around for weeks pretending to be Mallory on *Family Ties?*"

"No, that was fifth grade," Jennifer retorted. "Sixth grade was the year you walked around for weeks pretending to be Princess Leia."

Nora laughed. "You got me," she said. "Anyway, moving right along, what are you wearing tomorrow? No . . . wait, let me guess. That oversized rose-colored blouse you bought at the Sly Fox and never wear because you think it's *too* oversized."

"Actually, yes," Jennifer said. "And to answer your next question, yes, I am wearing it because of Moni. I mean, I got to thinking today that I must look pretty good in that color, too, since she and I have really similar coloring."

"You're both winters," Nora agreed. She and Jennifer had once figured out their color "seasons" with the help of an article in *Seventeen*. "What are you wearing the blouse with?"

"My black miniskirt."

"Have you thought of belting that blouse?" Nora asked. "Maybe with that black leather 'V' belt? It might help."

"Good idea," Jen said. "I'll try it. What are you wearing?"

Nora yawned. "The gray corduroy jumpsuit that Sally lets me borrow. I can tuck the legs into my boots. Unless it's warm. In that case, I'll probably wear a skirt."

"Not, by any chance, that challis skirt of Sally's, Nora?" Jennifer asked with exaggerated innocence. "You know, the one that looks sort of like Moni's?"

"No," Nora said, and changed the subject.

But after the girls hung up a few minutes later, Nora burst out laughing. She looked down at the long challis skirt she had been trying on when she called Jen. Yet another incidence of Jennifer/Nora mind-reading! Unfortunately, however, Sally was a good four inches taller than Nora, so the skirt looked ridiculous on Nora, even when she pulled it up practically to her armpits and covered it with a bulky pull-over sweater.

Just then, Nora's parents came up the stairs and stopped in Nora's doorway. They had been attending a reception at the Legal Aid offices where Mrs. Ryan was an attorney.

"*Bonsoir, cher Maman et Papa!*" Nora called.

A half-mile away, Moni was writing those same words at the top of a piece of French stationery. The paper was rimmed with soft, pastel-painted daisies, which reminded her of a field near home. And that made the tears of homesickness she thought she'd rid herself of the night before begin again.

"Stop it, Moni!" she ordered herself (in French, of course). "You are fourteen years old, not a baby! Why can't you look at this year as an adventure, the way Cameron did with his year?"

Suddenly, Moni brushed the tears from her face. "*Cameron,*" she nearly spat the name out. She wasn't going to think about him anymore. After all, it was partly his fault that she was in the mess she was in! Taking a deep breath, Moni decided to describe for her parents the bedroom she had all to herself in the Bryants' home. She looked around the room. She was getting used to it now. It didn't seem quite so bizarre and cold-looking as when she had first seen it yesterday.

"Hope you like the high-tech look," Mrs. Bryant had said, unlocking the front door. "The whole house is done that way."

"I love high tech," Moni had exclaimed,

without the foggiest notion of what the words meant.

Now she did. Everything in the entire house was either red, black, or chrome. Everything seemed to be square, with very sharp corners. And everything looked like it had come straight out of a science fiction movie Moni had seen a few years ago designed to show how ugly things were going to look in the year 2020! Several huge paintings, at least six feet by six feet apiece, hung throughout the house, but Moni couldn't make any sense of them. Each featured nothing more than a couple of sticks or a couple of circles or both against a stark background of — what else? — red or black.

Thinking about those paintings brought tears to her eyes again. How could the Bryants even call them paintings? To Moni, a painting was the kind displayed in Fleur's open-air marketplace by a local *artiste* who had painted the surrounding countryside in bright watercolors.

The decor wasn't the only reason Moni considered the Bryants a tad *excentrique.* Mr. and Mrs. Bryant, who had no children and were art professors at the local university, had a big boisterous German shepherd named Kitty and a crabby Siamese cat they called Pup!

But Moni wrote none of this to her parents. Instead, she exclaimed over how warm and friendly the Bryants were (which was true) and how spacious and private her bedroom was (also true). After all, she didn't want to appear ungrateful! Not after her parents had slaved for months to send Moni here because of her daily plea: "I want to try living in America!"

When the woman who waited on customers at the Gorgée family's tiny bakery had quit, Moni's mother had taken the job so they could save the wages they would have had to pay someone else. For a year her mother had stood behind the counter all day, never complaining, never admitting that she wanted more than anything to be at home taking care of Moni's two-year-old twin sisters. Moni and her two younger brothers were in school all day, so the babysitting duties had fallen to Moni's father. Papa, who should have been sleeping all day, since he had to bake all night!

She pictured Papa, coming through the front door every morning, just as she and her brothers were sitting down to breakfast. He would deposit a boxful of still-warm rolls on the table: basil rolls or potato rolls or dark rye rolls and on birthdays and Christmas, flaky croissants. Moni and her brothers would reach for the bread, cover it with fresh creamy butter, and wash it down with *un chocolat* — bittersweet hot chocolate. Papa would stand there, clutching his empty lunch pail, looking them over fondly. His clothes would be covered with a fine layer of flour dust, his chubby cheeks red from his half-mile walk home, and his eyes pouchy with fatigue. Still, he would always say, "It's another wonderful day, children!"

Moni covered her eyes, as if that could make the picture of Papa disappear. To think that she could be so disloyal as to paint him as a rich *bon vivant*, the owner of an international chain of French bakeries, no less! To think she had told *that* story when her parents had been worrying for years that a bakery chain would invade Fleur and set up an outlet that would put Gorgées' simple, tiny, and *only* bakery out of business. Not that *Moni* ever believed such a thing would happen. Fleur was too much in the middle of nowhere for a chain to consider. A village of 2800, it was two hundred miles from the nearest medium-sized city and not even remotely close to Paris.

Moni laughed humorlessly. She had told students at both Cedar Groves High and Junior High that Fleur was one of the "most exclusive suburbs of Paris." It was exclusive all right — so exclusive that no one from Paris lived there! Fleur was nothing but a hick town.

Hick town. That and *in the sticks* were two English phrases she'd learned from Cameron Carson. How many times had she heard Cameron use those phrases in the year he had lived with her family as a foreign exchange student? "It's Saturday night — isn't there *anything* to do in this hick town?" he would groan. Or "It'll probably be another ten years before the Indiana Jones movies make it out here to the sticks." Or simply (and most frequently): "My parents wanted me to get a taste of a foreign culture, but this is ridiculous!"

In the beginning Moni — who'd developed a huge crush on the tall, suave, handsome boy from Los Angeles the second he walked through the door — used to find herself actually apologizing to Cameron for Fleur's shortcomings, as if she were personally responsible.

Even now, almost two years later, Moni's cheeks burned scarlet at the memory of herself following him around like a lovesick puppy, hanging on to his every word. She remembered how she had ached with jealousy whenever she passed the bedroom he shared with Paul and Jean and saw the pictures of his six (six!) L.A. girlfriends on the wall. Each of these girls was very beautiful or at least striking in some way. The hair of one, for example, was green and purple and stood straight up!

The mail always brought at least two and sometimes as many as eight letters from these girls. Cameron spent very little time writing back, but that never seemed to discourage them. Usually, he would dash off just a few lines as he was eating breakfast. And one morning, in the second month of his stay, he had accidentally left one of these hurried notes on the table. Moni, both curious and jealous, had read part of it:

It's like time stopped in Fleur in the early part of this century and never started again. Take Monique, the oldest daughter. Yesterday, I asked her to define Porsche, Hackey Sack, and Bon Jovi. Pretty simple and universal terms, right? Well, she guessed that Porsche was a stew, hacky sack a Japanese car, and Bon Jovi some sort of candy! And I am stuck for a year with such simple-minded peasants!

Just then, Cameron had walked back into the kitchen, remembering his letter. Holding it in her hand, Moni had just looked at him, her eyes filled with tears.

Angrily Cameron had snatched the letter away and called her a *snoop*. Whatever that was, it sounded terrible to Moni, so she, too, had lost her temper.

"You are so . . . *méprisable!*" she had shouted, unable to remember the English word for "despicable."

"I wasn't being mean in that letter, I was being honest," Cameron had shouted back. "You are just *hopelessly out of it!*" She would never forget the sneer on his face.

After that exchange, they had spoken to each other as little as possible. Moni's parents noticed the coldness between the two, of course. In such a tiny house, it was very obvious when two people weren't getting along. But Monsieur et Madame Gorgée were helpless to solve the problem. They couldn't very well send Cameron away. After all, though it had meant feeding yet another mouth on their already tight budget, they had eagerly volunteered to house the exchange student. How their children would benefit, they had thought, by the presence of an American! What better way to help them improve the English they were learning at the town school?

For the rest of his stay, during those long, long meals when Moni and Cameron exchanged nothing but silent glares across the table and whenever she heard him belittling Fleur, Moni was making a promise. She would go to America and show them! She would show Americans that little Monique Bernadette Gorgée of Fleur could be just as sophisticated and worldly as they were! No American would ever make fun of her again!

And so, after sending her application to the foreign-exchange organization in Paris, she had embarked upon a secret campaign. Cameron had a subscription to the American magazine *Rolling Stone*, and covertly, Moni had studied and memorized each issue as if it were a textbook. When Cameron had finally returned to America, so had his *Rolling Stone* subscription, but Moni hadn't despaired for long. As luck would have it, her uncle, *Oncle* Damien, married a woman who had worked as a clerk in a boutique in Nice for twelve years. When this new aunt, *Tante* Jacquie, had heard that Moni had her heart set on going to the U.S., she had sent her a year's worth of *Seventeen* back issues from the boutique. Having bought boutique clothes at an employee discount for all of the years she'd worked there, *Tante* Jacquie had also sent Moni a huge boxful of clothes and costume jewelry (including the bell bracelets) she no longer wanted.

Every item of that clothing was at least three and as many as twelve years old, but each was at least colorful and "*boutique unique*," as Aunt Jacquie put it in the letter that accompanied the box. "Many of these clothes are out of fashion," the letter had continued, "but if you hang on to them long enough, they'll come back in style — even the bell-bottoms!" The "bell-bottoms" were denim pants that looked like regular jeans until you got to the bottoms of the legs, which were widely flared out. Moni thought they looked absolutely *absurde.*

But as for the rest of the stuff, Moni found that with a little judicious hemming, some creative mixing and matching, and a small investment in belts, pantyhose, and other inexpensive accessories, she had a new wardrobe that, while not what *Seventeen* was featuring, was at least . . . *chic unique*, Moni decided.

When she boarded the plane in Paris (her first airplane trip *and* her first trip to that city), she did so with an entirely new style, a new background, and a new and thorough knowledge of what was hot and what was not on *both* sides of the Atlantic Ocean. Many hours later, the pilot pointed out the Statue of Liberty, a gift from her country. Moni had looked out the window with growing excitement and whispered "They will not only accept the new me, they will *like* me, as well!"

She had seen almost nothing more of

New York, just the airport, as she changed planes. So it was not until she arrived in Cedar Groves that she got the biggest shock of her life: Not all Americans were like Cameron Carson.

Moni sat up on her chrome-and-red high-tech bed and rubbed her temples. "In fact," she whispered aloud, "I haven't yet met even *one* person like him."

She thought about the kids she'd met in Cedar Groves. They were friendly; they were curious. She'd overheard some of them complaining about having too much homework or bratty little brothers or that the fog was making their hair frizz. The fact of the matter was that, except for the language they spoke, these kids weren't all that much different from the *real* Moni! And most amazing of all, she suddenly realized, they had gone out of their way to be nice to her, to welcome her *even before she'd told them all those phony stories about herself*.

But now it was too late — she was in trouble! In her nervousness, she had gone ahead and told those stories. Nobody knew the *real* Moni.

The tears dripped down her face again. *Menteuse, menteuse*! Liar, liar! Nice as these people were, surely they would not tolerate a liar! They would drop her cold the instant they found out the truth, and she would be forced to spend a long, lonely, friendless year in Cedar Groves. Oh, why, why, *why* had she done it?

Moni jumped off the bed abruptly and headed for the closet, thinking hard. There was only one solution, she told herself as she donned one of the voluminous white flannel nightgowns her mother had made for her. She would have to keep something of a distance from these kids so that they would *never* find out the truth. She could do that while still being nice, couldn't she?

Yes, that was the only solution, she decided, folding back the covers on her bed. She would have to be a bit aloof. And by all means, she would have to stop offering details about her "jet-set" life unless she was absolutely forced to. Especially around that *très belle* blonde, Denise . . . the one who had been dressed in *très chic* clothes from head to toe!

Mince, alors! Darn it! Who would have thought that in this small town there would be a girl who actually lived the life Moni was pretending to live? Just with her knowledge of Paris, Denise could blow Moni's cover. The girl already seemed suspicious. Hadn't she eyed Moni's clothes suspiciously that afternoon? Moni bit her lip. Perhaps Denise had already guessed that Moni's skirt had been purchased way back in 1982.

Moni got into bed and turned off the big, ugly black lamp that looked more like a crane she had seen at a Cedar Groves construction site than a lamp. She sighed quietly into her pillow, feeling alone and lonely and worried about tomorrow. How she longed to hear the sweet little smacking noises the twins made as they slept in the bed beside her at home!

And then she remembered: Jason! Jason, with whom she had spent that oh-so-short minute before he'd had to rush off to a meeting. She would not have to be so on guard around him as with the others. For one thing, as her grandmother always said, boys weren't as suspicious as girls . . . or as smart! And then there was that other favorite saying of her *grand-mere*: Love conquers all! Even if Jason eventually found out the truth about Moni, it wouldn't matter. Love conquers all problems!

Smiling, Moni drifted into sleep, dreaming of red hair and freckles.

Chapter 4

Nora gasped. "Will you look at *that?*"

She was standing with Jennifer, Susan, and Tracy on the front steps of Cedar Groves Junior High the next morning before school. The other girls followed her gaze.

Wearing a Sony Walkman headset, Jason Anthony was jetting down the sidewalk on his skateboard. Monique Gorgée was running after him. And Tommy, Mitch, Steve, Andy Warwick, and Brad Hartley were running after *her.*

"Jason! Jason!" Moni called, panting. But because of the stereo headset and the skateboard noise, Jason was oblivious to her call.

"Hey, Moni Gorgeous, wait up!" Mitch and Tommy shouted after her. It was obvious she could hear them but was choosing to ignore them.

Eyes wide with shock, Jennifer nudged

Nora. "So Moni *didn't* see the light after she met Jason yesterday!"

"Actually, I think we've simply entered the Twilight Zone," Nora said in an equally surprised tone. She hoped the others couldn't tell how hurt she was that blond-haired blue-eyed Brad, whom Nora had gone out with, was running with the pack.

Mia Stevens approached the girls, but she had eyes only for the galloping Andy. "Look at him!" she said angrily. "What is his problem?"

Tracy sighed. "Moni Gorgeous."

Mia squinted at the fast-moving Moni. "Well, she *is* pretty. But I'd think Andy would find her . . . well . . . a bit *colorless* for his taste."

Jennifer and Nora exchanged a look, trying not to laugh. Mia was absentmindedly plucking at her spiky hair, which was the same lime green as the satin blouse she wore over tight leopard-skin pants. Mia and Andy were Cedar Groves' resident punk couple.

Susan pointed at Moni, who was wearing a yellow silk blouse and a paisley gypsy skirt, and then at Nora, in the gray corduroy jumpsuit. "If Moni's colorless," Susan said to Mia, "what do you call Nora?"

"Nora," Mia answered with a slight smile.

"You ought to take lessons from Mia in how to be tactful," Nora said to Susan.

"To be tactful is to be boring," Susan said with a yawn.

"Jason! Jason!" Moni called.

"Moni Gorgeous . . . wait!" the boys called after her.

Jason leaped off his skateboard, picked it up, and started up the stairs, taking them two at a time.

"Hey, Jason, Moni is trying to — " Nora began, but Jason zipped right past her. Loudly singing off-key to U2's "With or Without You," which must have been playing on his Sony, he didn't even glance in the girls' direction.

A pretty pout on her face, Moni stopped in front of the girls and watched Jason approach the school doors at a run.

"Oh, Moni, he just couldn't hear you with that stupid headset on," Nora said sympathetically.

"I've never seen him wearing a Walkman before, by the way," Jennifer said. "Maybe today is his birthday."

Moni's face brightened. "His birthday? *Splendide*! Then I must get him a present!"

Nora managed to squelch the sound she was dying to make — a gagging noise.

Meanwhile, the boys had stopped several feet away. Steve Crowley, truly perplexed, was running a hand through his dark, brush-cut hair. "Why Jason?" he asked the others.

Mitch and Tommy were shaking their heads, also totally bewildered.

"Maybe she doesn't know he's only in junior high," Andy suggested.

"See you in biology, Jason!" Moni shouted as the red-haired boy went through the school doors.

Andy sighed. "Scratch that theory."

"Well, I'm not going to just stand here crying about it with you guys," Tommy grumbled. "You know the old saying: 'Out of sight, out of mind.' I'm going to make sure I remain in that girl's sight so that I'll be the first guy she sees when she comes to her senses."

Tommy headed for Moni, and the rest of the boys followed on his heels. He boldly cut right between Moni and Nora so that he was standing directly in front of and not a foot away from the French girl.

Moni's eyes narrowed with anger. "Excuse *moi*," she said to Tommy with exaggerated politeness. "I seem to be in your way!" She backed away from him, gave the girls her charming little wave, then whirled around and stormed down the walkway that separated the junior high from the high school.

"I'm in love," said Steve Crowley, as

he and the other boys started off after her.

"Many people have told me I look like a Jon Bon Jovi with short hair," Tommy called after Moni.

She didn't even turn around. "Don't make me — how you say? — gag!"

The girls burst out laughing. But the boys continued to follow Moni, yelling "Hey, Moni Gorgeous!"

Finally she stopped, turned around, and stamped her foot. "You boys stop following me! I belong here" — she pointed at the high school — "and you belong there!" she pointed at the junior high. "Now stay there!"

The boys finally got the message. They stopped, huddled together, and stared after her mournfully.

The girls, except Tracy, were still laughing.

Tracy sighed. "I wish Steve Crowley would say he was in love with me!"

And I wish Brad would say that about me, Nora thought, surprising herself, but what she said was: "Steve? Not me!"

"Or me," Jen added.

"But he's so — how you say? — tall, dark, and handsome!" Tracy cried. "How can you guys be so casual about Steve?"

The bell rang and the group headed up the stairs.

"Easy," Nora said. "It's hard to feel

romantic about a guy you've known since kindergarten. Jen and I have been buddies with him since the days when —"

"Here we go again," Susan interrupted with a groan. "More best-friends-since-kindergarten tales! In today's episode, Steve Crowley puts mud down the back of Nora Ryan's blouse. Pul-leez, spare us!"

"Sure, why not?" Jennifer said with a giggle. "After all, these days you're telling the stories *for* us."

Inside, Jason was running down an upstairs corridor, casting fast glances over his shoulder about every fifty feet. Cool it, Anthony, he thought, coming to a screeching halt outside his homeroom. The French girl *had* to have gone over to the high school by now.

Jason plopped down at his desk. He was out of breath, and his gasping was attracting attention. Kids were staring at him as they filed into class. It was so uncool to run to class. It made everyone think you were worried about being late. Feeling very self-conscious, Jason held his breath in an effort to slow and quiet his breathing . . . but that just made it worse.

Finally Jason's breathing returned to normal. He tried to listen as Mr. Mario read a bulletin about an upcoming assembly. But he *still* felt like people were staring at him. He looked around. People *were* staring at him. And suddenly he understood why: They were no doubt wondering what gorgeous Monique Gorgée saw in him.

Well, so did he!

When the French girl had raced up to him after school the day before, no one had been more surprised than he! At first, he had thought it was some sort of trick, a trick that the other girls had put her up to. But when Nora and Jen had walked past him and Moni, they had looked as surprised to see Moni talking to him as he felt.

Jason almost groaned aloud. He hadn't handled it very well yesterday. Moni had stood there, smiling at him, telling him in her French accent that she wanted to get to know him better. He had been busy being terrified that he was going to blow it and say something really stupid. His only option, he had decided, was to get away from her before he did.

"I have to go," he'd interrupted her.

"Oh, no! Where?"

"To a . . . um . . . meeting . . . of my . . . um, skateboard club," he'd mumbled. What a lie! If Cedar Groves had a skateboard club, he sure had never heard of it.

Moni had looked so disappointed. "Oh! Well, some other time, yes? What is the name of your club?"

"The . . . uh . . . Skateboarding Scarecrows!" It was the first thing that had popped into his mind. How dumb. Jason had raced away from her, his face burning with embarrassment. He didn't want to stick around to hear her laugh at him.

But then, a few minutes later, he had heard her calling his name as he dodged out one of the school's back doors. "Jason, wait! I will walk to your meeting with you!"

Totally confused, he'd gotten on his skateboard and whizzed down the sidewalk at at least fifty miles an hour. After a block he was . . . safe!

But he'd thought about Moni for most of the evening. "*Why me*?" he kept asking himself. Sometimes he felt very pleased when he said it, sometimes he felt scared and his stomach hurt.

Mr. Mario was now droning on about peashooters being illegal on the school grounds.

Jason's mind remained on Moni. Maybe, he thought, it was just that all new people were nice to *everyone* at first. No, that couldn't be it, he decided, catching a glimpse of the golden head of Denise Hendrix, two rows up. When Denise had been new last fall and he'd introduced himself to her, she had acted as if he'd thrust a dissected frog in her face or something. (Wait a minute . . . maybe he *had*! He couldn't remember.)

Jason sighed and lowered his head till his forehead rested on his desk. He wasn't coming up with any answers about the Moni situation. He'd just have to keep avoiding her. Two reasons: (1) Whatever it was she was so crazy about, it was probably something that she *thought* he had going for himself, but that he really didn't; and (2) the minute she found that out, she'd lose interest and stop chasing him. And what guy in his right mind would want Moni Gorgeous to stop chasing him?

The bell rang, and Jason clamped on the Sony Walkman headset. What an inspired idea that had been! Wearing it, he had a logical excuse for not hearing Moni when she called his name.

Gingerly Jason stuck his head into the corridor and looked both ways. Then he ordered himself to stop being so paranoid. After all, the two people he needed to avoid were over at the high school: Moni, and his older brother Ed, who was unaware he'd "lent" his Walkman to Jason!

Chapter 5

When Nora and Jennifer walked into their biology class three hours later, Susan and Tracy were having a furious whispered fight.

"I say we tell her!" Susan hissed. "Now!"

"And I say we mind our own business!" Tracy whispered back. "After all, she isn't after one of the *normal* guys. One of the guys someone else might like, I mean." She blushed.

"Oh, so that's it," Susan snapped. "You're *glad* Moni's hung up on Jason and not competing for the so-called *normal* guys. I should have figured you'd have an ulterior motive." She stood up and took a step away from her desk.

Tracy reached out and grabbed her arm. "No!"

"What's going on?" Nora asked as she

and Jen set their books down on their lab table.

"Susan wants to warn Moni about what a disgusting personality Jason has," Tracy said, still holding Susan back. "And I say we shouldn't."

Nora and Jen looked across the room at Moni. Every time someone came through the door, the French girl looked up, eyes filled with hope. She was obviously waiting for Jason.

"I don't think we should say anything about Jason to her." Jen said thoughtfully. "I mean, she's probably spent some time with him by now, and she obviously doesn't think he has a disgusting personality. For us to say . . . well, that would be like an insult. Like we're insulting her taste."

The other girls nodded slowly.

"You're right, Jen," Nora said.

Susan sighed. "Yeah. I'll try to refrain from — how you say? — ah, yes, *barfing* when we are in the happy couple's presence."

Mr. Morris, the tiny, completely bald biology teacher, came through the door, clapping his hands. Jason slipped in right behind him. Without looking Moni's way, he went immediately to the lab table he shared with Tommy.

"Instead of our usual lab, we're going to spend the period discussing the upcoming

Fifteenth Annual Cedar Groves Junior High Science Fair," Mr. Morris said, passing out mimeographed sheets that contained all the details. "Doing a science project for the fair is strictly voluntary — "

"Then forget it!" someone called.

Mr. Morris looked up, an angelic smile on his face. " — but anyone who enters what I deem a satisfactory project in the fair will have his or her mark in this class raised one full grade."

"Bribe!" someone muttered.

"But of course," Mr. Morris said. "And if you already have an A average — all three of you" — he rolled his eyes — "you'll get an A-plus."

Nora looked around. Most students were sitting up straighter, obviously interested.

Mr. Morris clapped his hands again. "Please note that your project does not have to be biology-related. It can be in the area of chemistry, astronomy, physics, psychology, zoology, botany, *or* biology."

Jennifer's eyes lit up. "Zoology!" she mouthed to Nora.

"The list of last year's projects on this sheet demonstrates the wide scope of projects we usually have at our fair," Mr. Morris continued.

He went behind his desk and picked up three large boards that were hinged together. "This is the required project display format," he said, setting up the hinged boards on top of his desk in the configuration of a three-way mirror.

"Jeff will make ours for us," Jennifer whispered to Nora.

The class laughed when they saw the title of the sample project.

"WHO HAS MORE BODY FAT — 13-YEAR-OLD BOYS OR GIRLS?"

read the large letters at the top of the left-hand board.

"That's where your project title will go — and it must be in the form of a question," Mr. Morris said. He pointed to large letters reading "Hypothesis" on the bottom half of the same board. "Your hypothesis is what you *think* the answer to the question is before you've done any research or testing."

The teacher bent down and squinted at a piece of paper below the word "Hypothesis." "This student's hypothesis was that boys have a higher percentage of body fat than girls do."

Most of the boys in the class booed. The girls whooped and applauded.

Mr. Morris pointed to the middle board, which was headed "Methods." There were several snapshots on the board, plus a tool that looked to Jennifer like a wrench. "This part describes or illustrates how you went about doing your project. This young lady used a pair of calipers" — the teacher pointed at the wrenchlike tool — "to measure skin folds on her friends' upper arms and upper backs."

"I ain't got no inch to pinch," drawled a male voice from the back of the room.

The class laughed.

Mr. Morris pointed to the right-hand board, headed "Conclusions." "Finally, your results and conclusions. Here you will let us know if your hypothesis was correct." He smiled smugly. "In this case, the young lady was proved incorrect."

There were shouts of protest from the girls.

Still smiling smugly, Mr. Morris pointed to a chart under "Conclusions." "You can't argue with cold, hard facts, girls."

Several boys oinked their agreement.

"Who did that project, Mr. Morris?" Tommy called out. "I'll be sure to avoid taking *her* girlfriends out to eat. A guy could go broke."

The class laughed. But Tommy just smiled slightly, hoping Moni was getting the impression that he was a guy who did a lot of dating.

Mr. Morris clapped his hands to quiet the class. "Now, those of you who choose to do a project" — again, that sweet, innocent smile — "must submit its title for my approval by Monday. Remember, in the form of a question, please! Now, if you'll all take turns coming up here to look at the sample project, I'll answer any questions you might have. . . . "

For Moni, the rest of the period dragged by. When it was finally over, she flew out the door before the bell had finished ringing. And she didn't even glance at Jason.

"So her fever finally broke!" Tommy jeered at Jason. "That girl was *sick!*"

Moni raced down the street toward the Safeway. Why was lunch hour so terribly short in America? The lunch period was only fifty minutes long, and today she had only forty. She had promised Monsieur Armand she would come to his French class early to help a student who was falling behind. In Fleur, students had had a nice, leisurely two-hour lunch — enough to go all the way home and even have a nap, if they wanted one. But then again, Moni thought with a sigh, school in Fleur lasted until four-thirty.

She stepped on the mat that automatically opened the door at Safeway, then headed immediately for the in-store bakery on the far left side. There were several cakes on display in the glass bakery case, but only one — a small, rather plastic-looking chocolate devil's food — was within her price range. None of the cakes looked even remotely as tasty as those her father made, but there was nothing she could do about that right now. She was *désespérée*! Moni pointed out the chocolate cake to the clerk.

"Would you like me to write something on it for you?" the clerk asked.

"Yes, yes!" Moni said, and then she remembered that she had left her French/English dictionary in her locker. "Give me a minute, please. I must try to remember the English words I want!"

Meanwhile, in the cafeteria, Nora was studying the paper about the science fair that Mr. Morris had passed out. "Listen to what someone actually did as a science project last year," she said. " 'Can Eating Sugar Improve Your Test Scores?' " Nora bit off a piece of apple and shuddered. "I'm sure the answer to that was NO! See, after that initial burst of energy you get from sugar wears off, your energy and concentration levels actually sink lower than they were before you — "

"Can it, Doctor Ryan," Lucy said, waving a half-eaten Twinkie in her face. "Save it for med school."

Nora grimaced at the twinkie. "Enjoy

your coffin nail, Lucy. Sugar — white death!" she added in a ghostly shriek.

Susan groaned. "Pretend it's my birthday, Nora. And my birthday wish is that we have one lunch hour without a nutritional lecture from you."

"Speaking of birthdays," Jennifer said quickly, hoping Nora's feelings weren't hurt, "isn't that a cake box Moni's carrying?"

The others turned to see Moni standing in the cafeteria doorway on her tiptoes, surveying the crowd. It wasn't long before she spotted Jason's bright red hair at a big table with several other boys. The girls watched her hurry toward him.

Looking up, Jason saw Moni approaching. Fearing he would make a fool of himself in front of the other boys, he quickly stood up and went to meet her halfway.

"Jason!" she cried happily, swinging the cake box by its string in front of him. "For your birthday!"

He was speechless. Where on earth had she gotten the idea that today was his birthday? His birthday was in July!

Moni set the cake box on a nearby table and opened the lid to show him the cake. The words "For the best *épouvantail*" were crowded across the top of the cake in yellow.

"*Epou* — " Jason tried to pronounce the word.

"It is French for scarecrow!" Moni said with her husky laugh. "I could not remember that English word when I was at the bakery!"

"Scarecrow?" Jason echoed.

"Yes, yes! Your club — the Skateboarding Scarecrows! Surely you are the best one, no?"

Jason nodded dumbly. "No . . . I mean, uh, yes."

"Now, I must go to Monsieur Armand," Moni said regretfully. "I will see you after school, yes?" She rushed away without waiting for an answer.

Jason picked up the cake box and headed for the boys' table, passing the girls' table.

Nora stood up and peeked into the box as he walked by. "Moni gave him a cake!" she said to the other girls. "I bet she had it flown in from one of her dad's bakeries!"

"Maybe all the way from *New York*," Tracy said in a hushed voice.

By the time he reached the boys' table with the cake, Jason had recovered his confidence and found he was thoroughly enjoying the looks of awe on the boys' faces.

"What is an *épou . . . épou . . .*" Tommy tried, eyeing the cake.

Jason took a knife, cut off the part of the

cake with the French word on it, and began to eat it. He knew most of these guys had French next period, and he didn't want any of them to write down the word and look it up in Mr. Armand's hefty French/English dictionary.

"There is no one-word English translation for *épouvantail,*" Jason said airily. He paused dramatically. "But in France, an *épouvantail* is a man that women would die for."

The other boys were struck speechless.

Jason stood up and gestured at the cake. "Enjoy — with my compliments." And then, his own piece of cake in hand, he walked away, chin in the air.

"I just decided on my science project," Tommy finally muttered to Mitch.

"I thought you were doing 'Does Cigarette Smoke Retard Houseplant Growth?' " Mitch said. "You know, as a hint to your mom."

"That's my *official* project," Tommy said. "My unofficial — but just as important — project will be *'Why Jason?'* "

Every other boy at that table nodded and said, "Mine, too."

Chapter 6

The following Saturday, Jennifer knelt among a crowd of mewing, circling, rubbing cats inside the Cat Room at the Cedar Groves Animal Shelter. With one hand, she was dangling a bit of tuna over the dark-brown head of a Siamese kitten; with the other, she was gently pushing the other cats away. When the Siamese kitten raised his head and tried to take a bite of the tuna, Jennifer raised her hand higher.

She heard a knock on the window. Nora was outside, waving.

"Come in!" Jennifer mouthed.

Nora slipped in and shut the door quickly so none of the cats could get out.

"I can't believe it!" she said loudly over the meows of varying pitch. "Jennifer Mann, Cedar Groves' Save the Whales representative, weekly volunteer at the animal shelter, and all-around champion of animals everywhere, is actually torturing a kitten! Give whatever that is to him, for crying out loud!"

Jennifer giggled. "I'll give it to him, but he has to reach for it with a paw." And suddenly, the kitten did just that. With his right paw, he drew Jennifer's finger down so he could eat the tuna.

"*Splendide!*" Jennifer said. "That's three rights and three lefts for Chocolate Head. Mark it down for me, will you, Nora?" She gestured toward a clipboard on the floor.

Nora picked it up and read it aloud. "Spots? Puffball? Tiger? Fatty? Sneaky? White Boots? Gray Guy? Chocolate Head? Jen, what *are* you doing?"

"My science project," Jennifer said. She got up to get another piece of tuna from a can she'd placed high on a shelf near the door. "After we got off the phone last night, I came up with the perfect project for me — 'Are Cats Ambidextrous?' "

Nora looked at her blankly.

"Ambidextrous means — " Jennifer began.

"I know what it means," Nora interrupted. "It means someone who can use either hand equally well, instead of being right- or left-handed."

"Right- or left-*pawed* in this case," Jennifer said.

"Cute," Nora said. "I can see what your

methods are, but what's your hypothesis?"

"That they *are* ambidextrous. And guess what? So far I'm right! Look at the chart. Every cat I've tested here so far has used *both* paws about equally."

"You're talking about Spots, Puffball, Tiger, Fatty — "

"Right," Jennifer said.

"What dumb names."

"Thanks. *I* named them."

Nora laughed.

"Well, most of these cats were born here and were never given names," Jennifer protested. "And I wasn't going to just call them A, B, C, D, and so on. That's so cold. So inhuman."

Nora nodded seriously but her eyes twinkled. "Wouldn't want to be inhuman about animals, now would we?"

"Absolutely not," Jennifer said. "Anyway, I decided on this project because it demonstrates how it *is* possible to use animals for scientific purposes in a humane way. It also gives my test subjects a special treat. Between-meal tuna!"

"Are you also going to test cats who are actually owned by people?" Nora asked.

"Nobody can own a cat, Nora," Jen said. "They're much too independent. But yes, I will be testing cats who . . . well, I guess you could call them cats who have landlords."

Nora laughed and slapped her forehead in mock exasperation. "You're hopeless."

"I'm scheduled to do a bunch of cats who live with people on my block tomorrow — plus Furperson at Steve Crowley's," Jen continued. "And I'm going to call Mr. Rochester and ask him if I can visit Edna on Monday. Be thinking of other people who live with cats, okay?"

Nora nodded and watched her dangle a piece of tuna over the head of a huge tabby Jen marked down as "Big Guy." "Are you done with your work here?" Nora asked. "I mean, have you cleaned out all the cages or whatever it is they normally have you do here?"

"Yeah," Jennifer said. "We can leave as soon as I finish with Big Guy. Want to go somewhere?"

"I'm thirsty," Nora said. "Let's just walk down to 7-Eleven so I can get some grapefruit juice. I promise I won't gag if you buy a Slurpee."

"Or make any comments about junk food," Jennifer said.

"Junk *drinks*," Nora corrected.

With his left paw, Big Guy swatted at Jennifer's hand. "Speaking of junk food," she said, "are you still going to do your project on nutritious snacks?"

Nora nodded. "I've decided to call it 'Is There a Perfect Snack?' "

"If there is, it's probably some kind of complex carbohydrate," Jennifer said.

Nora brightened, "You're finally learning!"

"How can I help it with you around, lecturing me after every bite?" Jen muttered.

"*Moi?*" Nora asked with exaggerated innocence. "Well, you're probably right that the perfect snack is some kind of complex carb, like my homemade granola or some kind of pasta — "

"But that doesn't keep very well in a school locker," Jen interjected.

"Right," Nora said. "Pasta's out, granola's messy, granola bars have already been done. My perfect snack will have to be something that's nutritionally excellent, simple to fix, easily packable, storable in a school locker — "

"And probably totally *blah*-tasting!" Jen said, laughing.

A few blocks away, Moni, like Jen, was on her knees. She was in the Bryants' garage, helping Mr. Bryant paint bookshelves — black and red, of course.

A frazzled-looking Mrs. Bryant suddenly appeared in the doorway that led into the kitchen. "Oh, there you are, Moni," she said. "Honey, would you do me a huge favor and run down to 7-Eleven for a pint of sour cream? I'm right in the middle of a recipe, and I just realized I don't have half enough."

Moni stood up and brushed off her knees. She was wearing the ridiculous-looking denim bell-bottoms her aunt had given her, since she didn't care if she wore out the knees or got paint all over them. "*Oui*, Mrs. Bryant. I'll go as soon as I change my . . ." But the poor woman looked so *désespérée*. "I'll go right away," Moni corrected herself. After all, the 7-Eleven was only two blocks away. If she hurried there and back, no one would see her in the horribly outdated pants.

Shoving the money Mrs. Bryant handed her into her back pocket, Moni took off for the store at a trot.

"*Bonjour*, Moni!" she heard as soon as she got through the store's door.

Moni bit her lip to stop a groan. Nora Ryan and Jennifer Mann were standing in front of the magazine rack, flipping through *Rolling Stone*.

"*Bonjour!*" Moni called, scooting past them toward the dairy case. To her dismay, they followed her. She got the sour cream out of the case and turned around. Oh, she had just known it! They were staring right at the stupid bell-bottoms! Moni was sure they were about to burst out laughing.

"These bell-bottoms — they are the very

latest craze in Paris," she said haughtily before they could say anything.

To Moni, Jennifer looked very skeptical. "Then Princess Di probably wears them," Jennifer said. "I've heard that she's one of the first to jump on new French fashions. Have you met her, Moni?"

"Not yet," Moni mumbled. "She always seems to be out of the country with Charles whenever I am in London. Last time, they were in — how you say? — *l'Australie*. And now, I must go." Before they could ask her any more questions about her nonexistent jet-setter life, she whirled around and went to the cashier.

The girls watched her pay for the sour cream and leave. Then they headed for the cashier themselves.

"Moni sure doesn't believe in long, drawn-out good-byes, does she?" Jennifer said. "Sometimes she practically leaves in the middle of a sentence."

"But weren't those pants — how you say? — adorable?" Nora asked.

Jen nodded and sighed. "*Splendide*. I better start saving my allowance if I want a pair. I bet the Sly Fox'll get some next month. And I know my dad will never buy me any. You know him — he'll call them impractical. He'd probably worry that the bottoms would get caught in my *tricycle* or something!"

Nora smiled sympathetically. Whenever Mr. Mann bought Jennifer clothes, they looked as if he thought she was in second grade.

Jennifer turned to the cashier. "A medium cola Slurpee, please."

Meanwhile, Moni was flying down the street, nearly blinded by tears. She had really, finally blown her cover, she just knew it. She just knew that Jennifer and Nora hadn't believed for one second what she'd said about bell-bottoms! Jennifer had made that suspicious remark about Princess Di. And Nora had obviously been trying so hard not to laugh about the pants that she'd been unable to speak at all! Just wait till they spread the word. Come Monday morning, Moni was not only going to be the laughingstock of the entire school, she'd be shown up for what she really was, as well: a big phony! A big phony who was really so poor that she owned twelve-year-old castoff clothes!

Moni slowed down and then stopped. She didn't want the Bryants to see her crying. She was just sitting down on the curb when she heard . . . oh, no! *It couldn't be.* But it was! The *cluh-clack, cluh-clack* sound of skateboard wheels as they rolled over the cracks that separated each square of sidewalk. Yes, there he was, on the opposite side of the street, coming closer. Jason!

Moni jumped up and ran for home. How would she ever be able to bear it if *he* saw her in these *absurde* pants? Yes, surely he would hear about them on Monday and probably laugh his head off with everybody else. But Moni could not bear to see him laugh here, now, in front of her.

A half-block later, within a few houses of the Bryants', she turned to see if he was following her. No, he had gotten off his skateboard and was just standing there. Good! He hadn't seen her after all.

Moni took a deep breath and plastered a cheerful smile on her face as she walked up the Bryants' driveway. "But on the inside," she whispered to herself, "I am — how you say? — ah, yes . . . I am crying."

But Jason *had* seen Moni. In fact, when he first spotted her, sitting on the curb, his first impulse had been to dive behind the hedge of the house he was passing to hide from her and hope she hadn't spotted him already. Just before he had, however, to his utter shock, she had jumped up and run away. *And she had looked right at him before she did so!*

"Jason Anthony, you've lost your touch," he muttered to himself. And then he answered himself: "How can you lose something you never had?"

That was what had happened, he

guessed. Moni had finally discovered that Jason didn't really have whatever it was she'd thought was so great.

With a sharp ache of disappointment and regret, he watched her disappear inside the Bryants' house.

Well, it had been sort of nice while it lasted, he thought. But why was it ending *now*? After all, just yesterday afternoon Moni had chased him halfway home from school. Wearing the Sony Walkman and riding his skateboard he had, as usual, pretended he couldn't hear her forlornly calling his name.

What could have happened to change her mind between three P.M. Friday and three P.M. Saturday? There had been no slumber party, to his knowledge, on Friday night. So the other girls couldn't have ganged up and told her fifty stories about what a jerk he was or something.

Thoughtfully, Jason got on his skateboard and headed home.

It was as he was rounding the corner of Cedar Groves Boulevard and Fifth Street that it hit him: Maybe Moni had just given up on him because he never returned her interest. Yeah! That was it! That had to be it. Well, then, the solution was . . . he would have to show her he was interested. But how? How could he do that without spending a lot of time with her . . . a lot of time that would certainly reveal the *real* Jason? He couldn't do that. That would scare her away for good!

Jason was so lost in thought that he crashed into a mailbox and flew off his skateboard. "Watch where you're going, big guy," he muttered at it, unhurt but embarrassed. That's when his second brilliant inspiration of the day hit him: A *letter*. That was the solution to his problem! That was how he could keep Moni interested . . . at a distance.

He jumped up and patted the mailbox. "Thanks a lot, big guy!"

Two seventh-graders who happened to be passing by looked at Jason and then at each other. "Space cadet," one said, shaking his head.

Jason ignored them and patted the mailbox again. Who had ever cared what seventh-graders thought, anyway?

Chapter 7

Sunday evening, Nora was daydreaming, dawdling over her dessert in the dining room, when she heard the magic words, *bell-bottoms.*

She sat up straight. "What did you say, Mom?"

Mrs. Ryan sipped her coffee. "I said, now that people are buying Beatles' albums again and otherwise bringing the sixties back with a vengeance, next thing you know they'll be wearing bell-bottoms."

"I thought bell-bottoms were totally new," Nora said, wide-eyed. "So they were also in style in the sixties, huh?"

Her mom nodded. "Late sixties and half of the seventies."

"Oh, come on, Nora, you've seen the Rolling Stones wearing them on some of their really old videos, haven't you?" asked her older sister Sally.

"I guess I never noticed," Nora said.

"Your dad and I wore bell-bottoms in college," Mrs. Ryan said.

Mr. Ryan smiled at her. "Remember how we always had to clothespin the bottoms of those stupid pants so they wouldn't get caught in our bicycle spokes?"

Nora was bouncing up and down with excitement. "Those *stupid pants* are coming back in style, Dad! Moni, the French girl, has a pair, and she says they're the new hot thing in Paris."

"I can see Mom in bell-bottoms," Sally said, giggling, "but I just can't picture you, Dad."

Mr. Ryan tried to look offended. "I might have been a few pounds lighter in those days, you know."

"He looked great in 'em!" Mrs. Ryan cried. "I'll prove it." She dashed out of the dining room and came back with one of the twenty photo albums she kept on a shelf in the coat closet. Nora and Sally went and stood behind her chair as she flipped through it. "There!" Mrs. Ryan said, pointing.

Nora and Sally dissolved into loud laughter.

It was Mrs. Ryan's turn to look offended. "What's so funny? You girls better get used to the way bell-bottoms look if they're coming back in style like you say."

"It's n-n-not the bell-bottoms," Nora

panted, trying to stop laughing. "It's those *things* you and Dad have tied around your heads!"

Sally screamed with new laughter. "When you untied them, did your hair fall off? Looks like that was the purpose of whatever those are."

"Those are braided leather headbands," Mrs. Ryan sniffed, but Nora and Sally were laughing too hard to hear her.

"Well," Mrs. Ryan continued, "it just so happens that I still have that particular pair of bell-bottoms, and I was going to offer them to you, Nora, but — "

This time, Nora heard her. She gasped. "You still have them?" she interrupted. "Oh, Mom — "

" — but I never give presents to people who laugh at me," Mrs. Ryan continued, eyes twinkling.

"I'm not laughing anymore!" Nora cried, biting her lip and clapping her hands over her ears so she wouldn't be tempted to rejoin Sally in her loud ha-ha-has.

"You'd better not," Mrs. Ryan warned with mock sternness, "Follow me. They're up in the cedar chest."

Delighted, Nora danced from the room behind her mother, secretly turning around just once to share a final but quiet snort of laughter with Sally.

An hour later, Nora was talking on the phone with Jennifer.

" . . . I'm hemming them right now, and am I glad my mom's not as tall as Sally is," Nora said, cradling the phone between her cheek and shoulder as she pulled the needle through the soft denim.

"Oh, Nora, you're so lucky," Jen said with a sigh. "I found out from Jeff that bell-bottoms were really big in the sixties and seventies, just like you found out from your mom. But he doesn't have any for me to wear, obviously. He thinks I ought to check the St. Mark's thrift store to see if they have a pair someone might have donated years ago."

"*Splendide* idea. Then yours will be all soft and faded and broken in like mine," Nora said.

"And I'll be making a contribution to help homeless people," Jen added happily. "Want to go down with me after school tomorrow? Then we can wear our bell-bottoms together on Tuesday. If I can get some, that is."

Nora groaned. "Oh, Jennifer, I want to wear mine *tomorrow.* You can wear yours on Tuesday. Look, you'll still be way ahead of most people. I mean, the Sly Fox probably won't get any in for another whole month. I bet the boutiques in L.A. and New York aren't getting them in yet."

Jennifer sighed. "Okay, already. But it would have been fun to wear them on the same day."

"But then everybody would think we plan what we're going to wear to school the night before," Nora protested. "How sensible and *uncool.*" She giggled. "By the way, what *are* you planning to wear tomorrow?"

Blocks away, Jason plunked three books down on the desk in his bedroom and sat down in his desk chair with a satisfied smile. Who would have thought that the bookcase in the front hall, the one he had been walking by for thirteen years without a glance, would turn out to be a gold mine?

He'd gone down to it in search of an English/French dictionary. And not only had he found one of those, he'd also found a handy little item called a "thesaurus." With that book, you only had to look up a simple word like "shy" and it gave you an entire list of other words that meant the same thing but sounded a whole lot more sophisticated. But the bookcase's major treasure was a fat and dusty green tome called *The Greatest Poems of All Time.*

Jason picked up and reread the letter he had written to Moni just before going down to the bookcase:

Dear Moni,

I'm sorry I am so shy and/or busy when you're around. It's just that I have a lot of stuff on my mind lately. I want you to know that I think you're real pretty and nice and I like you even if I don't talk to you.

Sincerely,
Jason Anthony

Then he went to work with the thesaurus, crossing out words and writing new ones above them. The new letter read:

Dear Moni,

I regret that I am so reticent and/or preoccupied in your presence. My mind has been brimming with myriad deliberations of late. Be assured that I consider you very beautiful and kindhearted and I adore you from afar.

Sincerely,
Jason Anthony

Next it was time to put the English/French dictionary to use. He didn't think it was necessary to translate the entire letter; just a word or three, to add a bit of foreign flavor. Jason found the words he wanted and substituted them as he copied the letter over:

Ma Chère Moni,

I regret that I am so réservé *and/or preoccupied in your presence. My mind has been brimming with* innombrable *deliberations of late. Be assured that I consider you* très belle *and kindhearted and I adore you from afar.*

Sincerely,
Jason Anthony

P.S. Here is a poem:

Jason stopped and picked up the poetry book, feeling a little guilty. But he hadn't said "Here is a poem *I wrote*," had he? It wouldn't be his fault if Moni mistakenly got the impression he'd composed whichever poem he ended up including. And anyway, he was only going to choose one for which the author was unknown, one of the ones that said "anonymous."

A couple of hours and hundreds of pages later, Jason had rejected all but about five of the anonymous poems he came across in the book. Anonymous or not, many of the rejects just sounded too familiar. Others got a little too personal — talking about soft white necks and so forth. And some were just plain too mushy. Of the five acceptable poems, Jason settled on:

Time is
Too slow for those who wait,
Too swift for those who fear,
Too long for those who grieve,
Too short for those who rejoice;
But for those who love
Time is
Eternity.

Jason was sort of bothered by the fact that it didn't rhyme, but since it was in a poetry book it must qualify as a bona fide poem, right? His face also burned as he printed the word "love." But he wasn't, after all, saying he loved *her*. Still, he worried. Not so much about what Moni would think, but about what other guys would think if they got ahold of the letter and poem. Jason winced as he remembered the time, almost a year ago, that Charlie Parker had gotten his hands on a letter Randy Duckett had written to a girl. In a very exaggerated passionate tone, complete with dramatic pauses, Charlie had managed to read the entire thing over the school P.A. system before the principal could stop him. Ever since then, most of the guys had been calling poor Randy "Loveboat."

Jason ended up taking a fresh sheet of paper and copying the letter and poem once again, but this time he didn't sign his name. He signed it "Epouvantail." That way, if the letter ever got out of Moni's hands, he could always claim that one of the guys who had seen the cake had faked the letter out of jealousy, just so everyone would make fun of Jason.

"If I had really written that letter, I certainly would have signed my real name," he said huffily, aloud, rehearsing in the event of such a catastrophe.

He folded the letter and put it into an envelope, addressing it simply to "Moni." He would slip it into her locker tomorrow morning, before school. . . .

Wearily, Jason leaned back in his chair, stretched, and glanced at his clock radio. The digitals read 11:10. He'd been working on the letter for three hours! And now he wouldn't have time to start his science project: WHAT IS THE OPTIMUM WHEEL SIZE FOR SKATEBOARD SPEED? Being a man women would die for, Jason thought sleepily, was going to be a full-time job!

Chapter 8

On Monday morning, Moni dragged her feet along the sidewalk, head down. As she neared the junior high, she allowed herself one glance up. *Bon!* The front steps were empty. Her plan had worked. By coming to school with just a few minutes to spare, she was sparing herself at least one sure incidence of being laughed at. Certainly the news of her wearing bell-bottoms had spread by now . . . but maybe by the time she'd *have* to see the junior high kids — in biology — they would have forgotten about it.

Moni had just gone up the steps and was headed for the walkway that separated the junior high from the high school when she heard someone call her name. Reluctantly, she turned slightly and saw Nora Ryan running up the stairs after her. *And Nora was wearing bell-bottoms!* Moni stopped short, and her mouth fell open.

Suddenly Nora tripped and fell on the steps and the big stack of books she had been carrying flew in all directions.

Moni rushed back toward her. "Are you all right?" she cried.

Nora stood up, red-faced, and brushed off her pants. "I'm fine. But this is not my day already. First I overslept and now this. Guess I'm just not used to running in bell-bottoms. They sort of get in the way, don't they?"

Moni stood there, staring at Nora's pants. She just couldn't believe Nora was wearing them.

Nora grinned at her sheepishly. "Hope you don't mind about these. You know the old saying: 'Imitation is the sincerest form of flattery.' "

But Moni *didn't* know the old saying. In fact, she was so flustered she couldn't remember the meanings of the English words *imitation*, *sincerest*, or *flattery*. She mistakenly thought flattery had something to do with laughing. And that's how she got the idea that Nora had chosen to wear the stupid-looking bell-bottoms strictly as a show of support for Moni; just so that other kids wouldn't laugh at her. What a kind and *généreux* thing to do!

"Be prepared to see more of these at school," Nora continued. "Jen's going to try to buy some at the thrift shop this afternoon, and Tracy's mom is converting a pair of Tracy's regular jeans into bell-bottoms for her."

Moni was even more touched. This girl had even talked her friends into wearing the pants so that others wouldn't ridicule Moni!

Moni smiled warmly at Nora and then helped her collect her scattered books. She noticed that most of them were cookbooks.

"You use these in your cooking class?" she asked, handing Nora a book titled *The Salt-Free, Sugar-Free, Fat-Free, or All-Three Cookbook.*

Nora shook her head. "They're for my science project. I'm supposed to be developing the perfect snack, and I haven't even started yet. So I thought I'd better study these during lunch." Nora shifted the stack of books to one hip and looked at her Swatch. "Well, I'd better go. Only two minutes till the final bell."

Moni nodded, waved, and headed for the walkway, thinking about how much she liked Nora. She must suspect that all is not right with me, that all is not what it seems to be, but she is too nice to pry, Moni thought. Thinking back, she realized that of all the junior high girls she'd met, Nora seemed the least interested in Moni's supposed jet-set life. She asked the fewest questions about it and did the least amount of *ooh*ing and *ahh*ing. Moni liked that about Nora, too. What a natural, down-to-earth girl Nora was!

Impulsively, Moni turned around. "Nora, maybe I can come to your house and help you develop the snack!" she called to the American girl, who was just about to go through the doors of the junior high. "I know something about cooking and baking . . . because of my papa, I mean!"

Nora nodded. "Terrific! I'll call you at the Bryants' after school today."

Moni sighed happily and headed for her locker. Despite everything, it looked like she was going to have a real American friend after all!

A few hours later, in the boys' locker room, Tommy, Mitch, Andy, and Steve got into their gym clothes and loudly debated whether or not the referee had blown a call in the Cowboys-Browns game the day before. Secretly, however, they were keeping an eye on Jason. Finally, the red-haired boy tied the laces on his running shoes and left the locker room for the field.

The football talk immediately ceased.

"Okay, guys, we've got two minutes," Tommy muttered. "So let's approach this thing scientifically. Mitch, you start."

"Problem: What does Moni Gorgeous see in Jason?" Mitch said.

There was a long silence.

"Well, come on!" Tommy growled. "Who's got a hypothesis?"

More silence.

"Look, we're desperate," Tommy said. "Someone say something. *Anything*. I don't care how farfetched it sounds."

Steve sighed. "Okay . . . um. . . . Hypothesis: Moni likes skateboarders."

Andy and Mitch laughed.

Tommy waved his hands at them impatiently. "Wait a minute. That's not such a weird theory, if you think about it. I mean, after all, it's like that skateboard's permanently attached to his feet. Well, it is most of the time, anyway." The eyes of all four boys strayed to the skateboard that Jason propped up against his gym locker because it wouldn't fit inside. Then they looked at each other, wicked grins spreading across their faces.

"Method: 'Borrow' Jason's skateboard for a while to see if Moni loses interest," Steve said.

Tommy stood up, trying to keep a straight face. "Hey, isn't there a rule about skateboards not being allowed inside school buildings?" he asked in an innocent tone.

The other guys nodded.

"Then I better keep Jason out of trouble by putting this outside," Tommy said, going over to pick up the skateboard. He went out the locker room door for a few seconds and then returned empty-handed. "I put it outside, but it accidentally rolled under that big hedge by the door," he said in the same innocent tone. "You guys will remind me to tell Jason where his skateboard is, won't you?"

"Oh, definitely," the others said.

They headed for the door that lead to the playing field.

It was Steve's turn to strive for an innocent tone. "Gee, Tommy, I've already forgotten what it was I was supposed to remind you about."

"Me, too," said Andy. "What was it?"

"Sorry, but I don't have the foggiest idea, either," said Tommy.

Their laughter rang out across the playing field.

Jason need not have worried about his letter and poem getting out of Moni's hands. Since the minute she had found it in her locker that morning, it had literally not once been out of her grasp. In PE, Moni had even run the 440 with it clutched in her right hand and then, as she showered after class, she had held it in her teeth. And all the while she had floated around in a happy daze, forgetting to notice if people were laughing at her because of the bell-bottoms fiasco.

Jason cared!

Moni had proof . . . even if she could not understand a lot of the letter or poem. That was not Jason's fault — he was obviously so sophisticated and intelligent that it was only natural for him to use big words like "preoccupied" and "deliberations." Tonight, when she had time, she would look up those and the other words she did not understand. Meanwhile, she certainly understood the word *adore* — it was the same in English as it was in French. And as for *love* . . . well, that word was known throughout the universe!

During biology, Moni only had the chance to throw a few rapturous glances in Jason's direction, because, as usual, the busy boy did not make it to class until after the teacher did. At the end of that period, he left before the bell had finished ringing.

At noon, she searched the junior high cafeteria for him in vain. When she walked by the table where he usually ate, several of the boys sitting there whistled at her.

"*Bonjour*, Moni Gorgeous. Care to join us?" called Tommy.

She stopped. "Where is Jason, please?" she asked coldly.

Mitch put one of his arms around the chair next to him. "Sit down and we'll tell you," he said, gesturing at the chair with his chin.

Desperate to find Jason, Moni reluctantly pulled out a chair that wasn't right next to any of the boys and perched on the edge of it. "Okay, I sit. So tell me now."

Andy fingered the spike collar he wore around his neck. "Well, we can tell you that wherever he is, he's about four inches shorter than usual."

The other guys laughed. Moni wrinkled up her face at them, confused.

"And he's certainly not *board,*" Steve added.

Everyone at the table except Moni roared with laughter.

Moni's chair made an angry squeak as she pushed it backward and stood up abruptly. "You do not know where he is," she snapped. "You are so . . . so — how you say? — ah, yes, immature! And *une bande d'idiots!*" She stormed away, keeping her eyes peeled for red hair. Moni just had to tell Jason how *magnifique* the letter and poem were. Oh, where was he?

Jason had spent the first half of the lunch hour searching every square inch of the boys' locker room for his beloved skateboard. And now — trying very hard not to cry — he was on his way to the administration office to check the Lost and Found closet.

"It is strictly against the rules to bring a skateboard on campus, you know," Mrs.

Peters said sternly when he emerged from the closet empty-handed. "Are you sure one of the PE coaches didn't confiscate it?"

Jason shook his head sadly. "I asked every one of them."

Mrs. Peters showed no pity. "I hope you're aware that if someone finds it and brings it in to the Lost and Found, we'll have to confiscate it and send a note home to your parents letting them know you've broken a rule. And you'll have to bring the note back signed by one of them before we'll release the skateboard."

Jason trudged out of the office toward his next class. He was doomed. If someone did find the skateboard, Jason would get in trouble both at school and at home for breaking school rules. If it didn't turn up, he'd not only be skateboardless, he'd also have to beg his parents to buy him another one. And he'd probably have to promise three solid months of dishwashing or some such thing to pay for it. His future looked bleak no matter what happened.

After school that day, for the first time, he actually *walked* down the main corridor. He felt as if he were missing a leg or something.

"Jason!"

Oh, no! He threw a glance over his shoulder. Sure enough, Moni was running toward him. He had forgotten all about the letter and poem! And if he had ever felt less able to be witty, charming, and sophisticated, it was today when he was in mourning for his skateboard. Jason took off for the front doors at a run.

"Meeting!" he shouted back to Moni, by way of explanation.

"*Magnifique!*" she called after him. "It was *magnifique!*" She stopped, and her mouth drooped with sadness as she realized he hadn't heard her.

Moni was unaware that she had stopped right next to Tommy's locker, where he, Mitch, Andy, and Steve were gathered. As she walked away, the boys gaped at each other, speechless.

"*Magnifique?*" Steve finally managed to say to the others. "Jason walks like a duck . . . and she still calls him 'magnificent'?

"Let's review," Tommy said solemnly. "Problem: What does Moni Gorgeous see in Jason?"

"Hypothesis: Moni likes skateboarders," Mitch said.

"Method: 'Borrow' Jason's skateboard for a while to see if Moni loses interest," Andy said.

"Conclusion: It's not the skateboard!" they all shouted mournfully.

A minute later, still feeling very sad that she had been unable to thank and compliment Jason for his efforts, Moni passed Denise at her locker.

Denise shrugged into a Guess denim jacket and pulled a handful of long, shiny blonde hair out from behind the collar. She eyed the French girl with some surprise. First, because for once Moni seemed to be alone, without an admiring group of boys or girls tagging along after her. And second, because she looked so unhappy. Maybe, Denise thought, she had misjudged the girl. Maybe Moni *wasn't* out to become the most popular, envied, and copied girl in the entire school. And maybe everybody had finally realized that, except for her French accent, there wasn't anything particularly special or exotic about Monique Gorgée. So maybe, Denise concluded, it was time to be nice, time to make amends, time to become friends.

"Moni!" she called, heading after the girl.

Moni stopped and turned around. She waited for Denise to catch up. "Yes?" she said, and Denise thought she sounded suspicious.

"I just wanted to tell you how terrific you look in that shade of green," Denise said warmly. "By any chance, did you buy that sweater at Fossettes, that really exclusive boutique on the Champs-Elysées?

Jade is sort of their trademark color, you know."

Moni was regarding Denise with a cool little half-smile, but inside, she was panicking. So Denise had finally decided to blow Moni's cover! The question about Fossettes — which Moni had never heard of — was obviously a trap. Instead of a boutique, it was probably a seedy Paris thrift store or the French version of America's K mart! Well, she was not going to fall into Denise's trap by saying she shopped there!

"No," she snapped. "I bought it at . . . at Jubilé, one of the string of boutiques my *Tante* Jacquie owns throughout Europe and — " *Stop it, Moni!* she ordered herself. *Menteuse, menteuse!* Liar, liar! Here Denise was trying to catch her in one lie and Moni was adding lies on top of it! Quickly she turned and stomped off down the hall so Denise wouldn't see her distress.

Utterly shocked, Denise stared after her. And then she got furious. What right did Moni have to be so hostile to Denise? How mean of her to act so haughty and nasty when Denise was only trying to be nice! It was obvious the French girl saw Denise as a competitor. Moni was probably even jealous of her.

Tossing her head angrily, Denise headed for the main doors.

"Wait! Wait a minute!"

She turned around to find Jennifer, Susan, and Tracy running toward her.

"We need your opinion!" Tracy and Susan called.

Denise stopped and waited for them, thinking that whatever they wanted her opinion about, she'd also give them her opinion about a certain French girl.

But the girls flew right on by Denise, shouting "Wait, Moni! Wait a minute! We need your opinion!"

"Okay, Boney Gulp," Denise muttered, "if that's the way it's going to be, then this is war!"

Chapter 9

That evening, Jennifer left the Parsons' house, across the street from her own, with a half a can of tuna and a lot of doubts about her science project.

Calling "I'm back!" to Jeff and her little brother, Eric, who were watching TV in the family room, Jennifer went into the kitchen. She stretched a piece of plastic wrap over the tuna and put it in the refrigerator.

"So what was Slinky Parsons?" Jeff asked, coming into the kitchen. "Right-pawed, left-pawed, or ambidextrous?"

Jennifer sighed. "Right. Except for Mr. Rochester's cat Edna, who's left-pawed, the last ten cats I've tested have been right-pawed."

"And your hypothesis was that cats are ambidextrous?"

"Uh-huh."

Jeff tugged at a lock of Jennifer's long

black hair. "Don't be so upset. So your hypothesis was wrong. So what? That's the whole purpose of a science project — to test a theory. Your conclusion will just be that your hypothesis was wrong and that most cats are right-handed — uh — pawed."

Jennifer sighed again. "But I can't say that, either," she said. "All of the cats I tested at the animal shelter were ambidextrous. That's the whole problem. There's no rhyme or reason to any of this. Some cats are ambidextrous, some are right-pawed, and a few are left-pawed. My conclusion is going to be that there is no conclusion! It's turned out to be a stupid project."

Jeff patted her arm. "Now, Jen, it's not a stupid project."

"It is, too!" Jennifer wailed. "Mr. Morris said we'd get upped a full grade for doing a satisfactory project, but I just know he won't find mine satisfactory."

"He will, too," Jeff said. "Especially when he sees how much work you've put into it."

Shaking her head, unconvinced, Jennifer went up to her bedroom and pulled out her diary, prepared to pour out her misery to it.

Impulsively, however, she picked up the phone and called Nora. What I need right now is cheering up, not writing down! she thought with a wry smile.

"*Allô!*" she said when Nora answered the same way. Jen could hear pots and pans clattering in the background. "Are you in kitchen?"

Nora giggled. "No, Brainy. I'm up in my bedroom holding a rehearsal of my all-cymbals band. And a one, and a two, and a. . . ."

"Cute," Jennifer said. "Guess what? Jeff took me to the thrift store after school today and I got a pair of bell-bottom jeans for only four dollars! They're really cute — there's a little heart patch on one knee to cover up a hole. And Nora, the thrift store had two more pairs. We could tell Lucy about them or maybe Amy or — "

She was interrupted by a loud squeal and then a burst of low-pitched, familiar-sounding laughter.

Nora started laughing, too. "Jen, I've gotta go. Moni just sifted my science project onto the floor."

"Moni? Moni's there?"

"Mmhmm," Nora said absentmindedly. "Didn't I tell you at lunch that she offered to help me with my project?"

"No, you didn't."

"Well, this girl turns out to be a whiz at baking . . . but she's not terribly familiar with American utensils and appliances — ”

Jennifer heard a loud mechanical growl and then a shriek from Moni.

Nora roared with laughter. “You have to run the water with the garbage disposal, Moni!”

Jen said good-bye and hung up, unsure whether Nora heard her or not. She picked up her pen and opened her diary.

Moni is over at Nora’s tonight, and it sounds like they’re having a really good time, she wrote. *Moni’s been sort of aloof to everyone . . . nobody’s been able to get close with her. Until now, I guess. She obviously likes Nora or she wouldn’t have offered to help . . . and Nora thinks Moni is great. So it looks like they’re becoming friends. I’m glad for them.*

She threw her pen down, flexed the fingers of her writing hand, and stared for a long minute out the window into the cloudy, starless night. Then she picked up her pen again.

But if I’m so glad, how come I feel more depressed right now than I did before I called Nora?

Over at the Ryans’, Nora was explaining the finer points of garbage disposal operation to Moni.

"First, you shove the junk down there," she said, pushing several zucchini peels into the drain. "Then you turn on the water, and *then* you flip on the disposal." She giggled. "The disposal is a pretty powerful thing, but it can't reach up and get the stuff that's sitting in the sink," Nora shouted over the grumbling and crackling of the disposal.

Moni giggled, too.

"I'm surprised you've never used a garbage disposal before," Nora said, switching it off and facing Moni.

Moni took one look into Nora's friendly, puzzled eyes and suddenly felt an overwhelming urge to confess everything to her. *The truth is*, she wanted to say, *nobody in Fleur has a garbage disposal. Not even the mayor, let alone the town baker and his family — my family — who live in a tiny cottage straight out of another century, according to an American boy named Cameron Carson.*

She took a deep breath. "The truth is — "

"The truth is, you never operated a garbage disposal because you had a maid or cook or housekeeper to do it for you," Nora interrupted cheerfully. "I forgot about how rich your family is."

Moni clamped her mouth shut.

Nora misread her expression. "Don't be

embarrassed. If *we* had a cook or a maid or a housekeeper, I would be absolutely thrilled and proud of it." She grinned and then made a lofty gesture toward an imaginary person. "James, bring us some tea on the veranda, please," she said in a veddy veddy snooty English accent.

The timer went off. Nora put on a padded mitt and pulled a cake pan out of the oven. "Voilà!" she cried, setting it with a flourish on top of the stove. "The first batch of Zucchini Bread Squares supplemented with calcium, rose hips, and wheat germ."

The girls sat down at the kitchen table, giving the concoction a few minutes to cool.

"Are you still crazy about Jason Anthony?" Nora asked, struggling to keep a groan out of her voice.

Moni beamed. "Oh, yes! And he is crazy about me. Today, he wrote me a love letter and poem." She pointed to a folded-up piece of paper tucked in the sleeve of her jade sweater. "I would read it to you, but it is too — oh, how you say? — ah, yes, personal."

Nora stifled a burst of laughter. Jason had written a love letter? It was too — how you say? — ah, yes, gaggable. It was too gaggable for words. "How nice," she managed to mumble, biting her tongue and remembering what Jen had said: To express disgust about Jason would be to insult Moni's taste in guys.

Nora jumped up, went to the stove, and cut the bread into three-by-three-inch squares. She put two of the squares on plates and brought them over to the table. Nora and Moni took big bites, exchanging hopeful looks. The girls chewed silently for almost a minute.

"Well," Moni finally said, "it *is* perfectly nutritious — "

"And perfectly awful," Nora said, giggling. "It tastes like lumpified sawdust. I guess we'll just have to try, try again."

This time Moni jumped up from the table. She took the pan of bread and headed for the sink, grinning at Nora. "I think I will practice with the garbage disposal!"

When Jason walked into the boys' locker room the next day before PE, he found, to his utter delight and amazement, that his skateboard was propped up against his gym locker. He picked it up gently, lovingly, and wanted to kiss it! But he stopped himself just in time, remembering that he wasn't alone in the room. He could imagine what some of the guys would say if they caught him doing it! "*Jason Anthony is better with fiberglass than he is with French girls!*"

Jason suspected that one or more of his

pals had probably taken the skateboard as a practical joke. He glanced over at Steve Crowley's locker, where Steve, Tommy, Mitch, and Andy were having a loud argument. Something about the words to a new Mötley Crüe song. That's funny, Jason thought. If they had taken the skateboard yesterday, wouldn't they be watching me right now to see my reaction on getting it back?

Shrugging, Jason finished getting into his gym clothes and left the locker room, waving to the guys as he passed them.

Tommy waved back absentmindedly. "The guy is saying the word 'pace' not 'pays,' " he said to Mitch. "I ought to know. I've listened to that song about twenty times already."

The instant Jason went through the door, however, the boys dropped the phony argument.

"Okay," Steve said, "I did a lot of thinking about the Moni-Jason situation last night, and I came up with another really good theory. You know how before Jason always — "

Tommy held up a hand. "Wait! Let's use the scientific approach. It's more efficient. Problem: Why is Moni Gorgeous crazy about Jason?" He nodded at Steve.

Steve grinned. "Hypothesis: She doesn't know what a jerk he is. Yet."

The others stared at Steve thoughtfully.

"Have you noticed how he's been on his best behavior since Moni came to this school?" Steve continued, running an excited hand through his dark, bristly hair.

Andy nodded slowly. "Come to think of it, you're right. He hasn't been hassling the girls at lunch . . . making stupid remarks in class . . . Jason Anthony just hasn't been Jason Anthony."

Steve nodded vigorously. "You know why that is? I think it's because he doesn't want Moni to see what a jerk he really can be, and he's never really sure when she's going to appear on the scene. I mean, she comes over to our cafeteria at lunch a lot . . . but never at the same time, right? Sometimes she comes looking for him right at the beginning of lunch, sometimes it's not till right before the bell, and sometimes — "

Mitch slapped a fist into the palm of his hand. "Gotcha. We need to have Moni catch him in the act . . . in the act of being a jerk, I mean. But how?"

"I think Jason would act like his normal self if he was a hundred percent sure Moni wasn't going to show up," Steve said. "And it just so happens she can't possibly come into the cafeteria today. She has a dentist's appointment during lunch, and he knows it. Didn't you hear her yelling that at him when he ran out of biology this morning? He was really in a rush to get somewhere."

Tommy heaved an exasperated sigh. "How's she going to see him acting like a jerk in the cafeteria if she's not there, Genius?"

Steve flashed a confident smile and reached into his gym locker. "With this," he said, holding up a small 35mm camera.

Mitch and Andy slapped Steve on the back. "All right, guy!" Andy said. "Good going!"

Tommy took the camera and looked through its viewfinder. "Smile, Jason," he said with a wicked chuckle. "You're about to be exposed."

Chapter 10

At noon that day, Jason skateboarded toward the cafeteria, feeling carefree, happy . . . and like his old self! What a good day it was turning out to be. First, he'd gotten his skateboard back. Second, he had a whole Moni-less lunch hour to look forward to. A whole hour in which he wouldn't have to worry about blowing it in front of the French girl.

To celebrate his new freedom, Jason immediately headed for the girls' table and told Lucy Armanson that the government was planning to crack down on hot dog manufacturers because of all the "insect parts and rat hairs" that had been found in them.

"Oh, gross!" Lucy shrieked, spitting a bite of hot dog into her napkin. "Get out of here, Jason!"

Nora laughed. "That'll teach you to eat

hot dogs, Lucy. The worst part is they're also filled with nitrites. Ugh!"

Nora didn't laugh for long. Jason's next trick was to stick his finger into the carton of blueberry yogurt she'd been eating. Face pinched with annoyance, Nora tried to swat at his hand, but he raised it to his mouth and licked his finger.

"Thank you, but I prefer peach," he said.

"Get out of here!" Nora cried. Then, all of a sudden, her expression changed. "Why don't you go away and write a few more *love letters*, Jason?" she said loudly. She started to make kissy-kissy noises, and Susan, Lucy, and Tracy joined her.

Alarmed, Jason glanced over at the boys' table. Had they heard what Nora said? But none of them were looking his way except for Steve Crowley, who was standing up and aiming a camera in the direction of the girls' table. Jason headed for the boys' table. Though the boys didn't seem to be paying any attention to him, he was still worried: If Nora had heard about the letter and poem, maybe the boys had, too. Better check.

To his surprise, they were again arguing about the words to the same Mötley Crüe song. Jason sat down next to Tommy and opened his lunch sack as the conversation shifted to last week's Cedar Groves High

School football game. He took a big bite of his tuna salad sandwich and looked over at the girls' table. Nora and Lucy were looking right at him and nodding, apparently agreeing with something Susan — who looked disgusted — was saying about him. Jason was so relieved the boys weren't making fun of him that he set down his sandwich, inserted a pencil into each of his nostrils, and grinned widely at Nora and Lucy as the pencils dangled in front of his teeth. But before he could see the girls' reactions, Steve popped up right in front of him and snapped a picture with his camera.

The football talk suddenly stopped. Tommy, Mitch, and Andy laughed and called, "Way to go, Crowley!"

Jason stood up and took a swipe at the camera, trying to grab it away from Steve. But Steve — who was a lot taller than Jason — held the camera out of his reach and moved away from the table. "See you guys later!" he called over his shoulder. "I'm going to lock this priceless film in my locker until I can get it to one of those sixty-minute places after school."

"What's going on?" Jason asked angrily.

"Don't worry," Tommy said in a falsetto. "With those pencils as accessories, you looked so — how you say — ah, yes, suave. You looked so suave!"

Instantly, and with a sinking heart, Jason realized what the boys were up to. Tomorrow, Moni was going to get a true picture of Jason!

Meanwhile, the girls were discussing Jason's latest antics with much indignation.

"Remind me never to borrow a pencil from him," Susan said.

"I just wish Moni had been here to see him in action today," Tracy said.

Nora took a sip of her cranberry juice. "But don't you see? That's why he acted the way he did today . . . because she *wasn't* here. He wouldn't dare act that way if she was."

"Too bad we can't get her to have lunch with us," Susan said. "Imagine, no more food contaminated with incurable cooties."

"Really," Nora said, giggling. "Actually, though it wasn't for that reason, I asked Moni to eat with us today. She wanted to but she had a dentist appointment."

Jennifer tried to catch Nora's eye. She wanted to see how disappointed Nora was that Moni hadn't been able to join them. But Nora was looking the other way.

"Speaking of Moni," Nora continued, doesn't she look adorable today in that little brown corduroy jumper? I never would have thought to pair that with a pink turtleneck sweater and pink tights . . . but it all goes together just perfectly."

Denise had arrived at the table as Nora spoke. She was wearing a red denim miniskirt and a matching beret, under which all of her hair was tucked. Jennifer thought she looked every bit as adorable today as Moni did. But as far as Jen knew, no one had bothered to compliment Denise. "You look adorable, Denise," she said loudly.

Denise smiled her thanks and sat down beside Jennifer.

"Ooh, a French fashion magazine!" Tracy cried, grabbing it from the top of Denise's stack of books.

"I don't want to hurt anyone's feelings, but I felt I had to do something when I found out Moni has you all wearing — or trying to get — bell-bottom jeans," Denise said, taking the magazine back from Tracy. "This magazine just came out three days ago, and it's airmailed from Paris to our house." She flipped through the issue until she came to a story that was illustrated with a picture of a girl leaning against a street sign wearing straight black denim jeans and a black T-shirt. Denise pointed to a paragraph. "Read this aloud," she said to Jennifer.

Jennifer took the magazine and looked

at the paragraph. "But it's in French! I only know a couple of these words."

"Oh, yeah, I forgot about that," Denise said, taking the magazine back. "I'll translate: 'The sixties craze, according to France's top designers, has been dead and buried for about six months now. Many fashion-conscious women have expressed profound gratitude that one sixties style that did not make a comeback was bell-bottom jeans. Among that pants style's other faults, explains popular Left Bank designer Rian Rocheleau, it made short women look shorter.' " Denise allowed herself one quick glance at Nora before going on. " 'Speaking of denim,' " she continued, " 'today's most chic Parisienne teens are wearing straight, plain, five-pocket jeans. . . .' " Denise looked up. "The rest of this isn't that interesting."

Nora's face was bright red with anger. "Just what are you getting at, Denise?"

"That Boney Gulp seems to be purposely misleading you about French fashion," Denise said, "Probably just so she can have a laugh, at your expense, with her Parisienne pals."

"I bet you made up what you just read," Nora snapped, "knowing that we wouldn't be able to translate it."

Denise closed the magazine and tossed it across the table at Nora. "You don't believe me? Take it to Mr. Armand. Have him translate it for you. Page forty-six."

Nora stood up and tossed the magazine back at Denise. "You're hateful."

Denise's eyes narrowed. "I am not! I'm doing you a favor. I'm just warning you that she's trying to make you look ridiculous. Look at it this way: If bell-bottoms are really that hot, why isn't Moni herself wearing them to school? That's the biggest tip-off right there. You ought to be thanking me, Nora, not yelling at me."

"I'm not yelling!" Nora yelled. "And you're not only hateful, you're *wrong*!" She gathered up her books. "Moni's too nice to do a thing like that. She's not as calculating as *some* people I know."

Lucy cleared her throat. "Denise, did it ever occur to you that that magazine just might be a little behind?" she asked. "Maybe the bell-bottoms fad is so new that the magazine hasn't heard about it yet."

Denise shook her head. "*Nouveau* magazine doesn't just report on fashion, it *sets* fashion," she said disdainfully.

Nora picked up her books and pushed her chair away from the table. "Excuse me, but this short-and-getting-shorter girl has better things to do than sit around and listen to a perfectly sweet and innocent French girl being insulted." She flounced away toward the cafeteria door.

Jennifer stood up, prepared to follow her, then stopped. Maybe Denise was right. Maybe the French girl *was* simply trying to make them look ridiculous. After all, the truth was right there in the magazine, in black and white. And then there was something else holding Jennifer back . . . something that got stronger as she watched Nora march angrily toward the exit. It was a deep pang of jealousy. Jennifer couldn't remember Nora ever defending her or anybody else so vigorously.

As Jennifer stood there, Denise was looking at her bell-bottoms, the ones with the little heart patch on the knee. "I always keep a spare pair of jeans in my locker if you want to borrow them and change after lunch," Denise said to her.

"Okay, thanks," Jennifer said softly.

After school that day, Jennifer went to use the pay phone in the administration office and then hurried to the main corridor, hoping Nora hadn't left school yet. Jen sighed with relief when she spotted Nora still at her locker, putting on her jacket . . . then felt a twinge of her lunchtime jealousy when she saw that Moni was with her. In all of their afternoon classes, Nora had been nice to Jennifer but sort of preoccupied. She hadn't even seemed to notice Jen was no longer wearing the bell-bottoms.

"Hi, Nora. Hi, Moni!" Jen cried, forcing more cheerfulness into her greeting than she actually felt. "Nora, remember when you said you'd go to Lucy's grandma's with me to test Dazzle, her cat? Well, I just called her and she said you and I could come over this afternoon. She says she's been hoping you and I would visit her, but I think she especially means you." Mrs. Armanson was a retired nutritionist, and she and Nora enjoyed talking shop.

Nora groaned, but it sounded fake to Jennifer. "Oh, Jen, I'd like to, but I can't. I've just *got* to work on my own project. I'm bribing Moni here with a hot fudge sundae at Temptations. Then she's going to help me experiment again at my house — straight through till ten o'clock, if we have to."

Jennifer's face fell. "Since when did you start eating ice cream? I mean, what about the sugar and fat content you're always screaming about?"

Nora laughed. "I'm not eating it — she is." Nora pointed at Moni, who flashed Jennifer her neutral little half-smile. "I'm just buying it," Nora said.

"That still means you approve of it," Jennifer snapped.

Nora's eyebrows shot up in surprise at Jennifer's outburst.

Jennifer tried to make her eyes communicate for her: Oh, Nora, this has nothing to do with ice cream. Can't you see I'm jealous?

But Nora said nothing, just continued to look puzzled. There was a long silence.

"Look, Jen, why don't you just come with us?" Nora finally said.

Jen was unaware that Denise had approached the group and was standing behind her.

But Moni saw her. The French girl had no problem with Jennifer coming along, but she was suddenly afraid that Nora was going to include Denise, too. And Moni sure didn't want to give Denise more opportunities to trap her, to blow her cover.

"No," Moni burst out, "then I won't be — "

"Forget it, I can't go anyway," Jennifer said quickly, glaring at Moni. "Didn't you hear me before, Nora? I have an appointment with Mrs. Armanson. I, for one, try not to let people down."

Moni blushed as she realized that Jennifer thought it was *Jennifer* Moni objected to. But there was obviously no way Moni could set the record straight without revealing everything. "Maybe you could come over to the Bryants' soon and test their cat," she said in an effort to make amends. "They have a cat named Pup."

Jennifer tossed her head angrily. "No,

thanks. I don't think a cat named Pup would make a very good subject. He's probably mixed up about a lot of things."

Nora was alternately shooting helpless looks at Jennifer and glares at Denise. She was still angry about Denise's comments at noon.

"I'll go over to Mrs. Armanson's with you, Jennifer," Denise said.

"Fine," Jennifer said, finally realizing that Denise was standing behind her. She turned on her heel and headed for the main doors with Denise.

"I am so upset I can hardly see straight," Jennifer muttered once they were out of Nora and Moni's earshot.

"I know, and I don't blame you," Denise said gently. "I think she's not only trying to steal your best friend, she also wants to keep Nora all to herself. Did you see that look on her face when Nora asked you to go with them?"

Jennifer nodded miserably. "Denise, she isn't trying to steal my best friend — she *has*. Oh, go back to France, Moni Gorgée! Go back to France, *Boney Gulp*!"

Chapter 11

Jason Anthony was desperate. That same afternoon, he paced his bedroom frantically. He was sure the boys planned to spring those pictures on Moni tomorrow, and he needed to take desperate action to counteract them. As he paced, mulling over various ideas, his eyes kept straying to the big green book of poetry on his desk. You'll have to send her one of those really mushy poems you rejected the other night, a little voice inside his head kept saying. "No!" he kept answering it aloud.

But finally, the little voice won. With a sigh, Jason went to his desk and began to flip through the Anonymous section of the chapter in *The Greatest Poems of All Time* called "Poems About Love." He found the perfect poem right away and begin to copy it onto notebook paper:

*Black Is the Color of My
True Love's Hair*

Black, black, black is the color of my
true love's hair,
Her lips are like some rosy fair,
The prettiest face and the neatest
hands,
I love the ground whereon she stands.

The poem had three more stanzas, but Jason decided to leave them out. One of them talked about "mourning and weeping," and he thought that was going too far.

"But the stanza I'm using goes too far, too." Jason groaned after rereading what he'd written. It was so mushy and weird — what *was* a "rosy fair"? Worst of all, Moni would have it in writing that Jason considered her his "true love."

But Jason bit his lip and forced himself to sign the poem "*Epouvantail*" with a flourish. After all, he was desperate.

Meanwhile, having just entered Temptations, Moni was looking around with disappointment. The place reminded her of the Bryants' house — lots of metal and wall-to-wall mirrors. In addition, there were some blue neon words hanging on the walls — words that didn't seem to have anything to do with ice cream — and they made the place look even more unfriendly and cold.

Moni sighed as she and Nora sat down at a table. "This high-tech look I see so much in America . . . it is ugly."

Nora nodded. "I'm getting a little tired of it myself."

"When you said ice cream shop, I guess I expected something like what we have in Fleur," Moni said wistfully. "There, Mrs. Balmot, who owns the little drugstore, has put two tables outside under the awning. And if you sit down at one of them, she brings you a dish of *glace* that is so soft and creamy" — Moni glanced at the bowls of ice cream a Temptations waitress was carrying past the table — "not hard and in balls like you get in America."

"You can order frozen yogurt here," Nora said. "It's soft and creamy."

Moni realized that she had sounded ungrateful. "I am not saying that French *glace* is better than American *glace*. It is just different."

Nora smiled and signaled to one of the waitresses.

Moni couldn't keep herself from reminiscing about home. "When you sit outside Mrs. Balmot's with your *glace*, everyone stops to chat. Like the — how you say? — *facteur*?"

"Mailman," Nora said. "Wait, that's sexist. My mother and father would kill me if they heard it. Make that letter carrier."

"Letter carrier," Moni repeated. "The letter carrier stops to chat, and so does everybody else you know who is walking by — " She stopped herself suddenly, realizing that the entire setup sounded terribly, suspiciously "hick town"! She glanced at Nora in alarm.

But Nora was staring dreamily over Moni's shoulder. "Oh, Moni, it sounds so romantic, so . . . *European*."

Moni giggled with relief. "Sometimes, after I got home from school, I would take my twin sisters there. Mrs. Balmot would come out and scold them while trying not to laugh at the *spectacle* they always made. '*Mes enfants*,' my children, she would say, '*glace* is for eating, not for wearing!' And then — " Moni's voice broke and her eyes filled with tears as she pictured the twins and their happy, smeared little faces.

Nora reached across the table and squeezed her hand. "Oh, Moni, you're homesick."

Moni dabbed at her eyes with a napkin. "Yes. I am sorry. Please don't be angry with me."

Nora gasped. "Angry? Why in the world would I be angry?"

"Because you've been so nice to me . . . everyone has been so nice to me. I have no right to be homesick."

"Oh, Moni, you're wrong. You have every right to be homesick. Listen, I was homesick when our class went to Washington, D.C., for a few *days*. And here you are spending months in a totally different country. How could you possibly think I wouldn't understand?"

Moni kept her eyes on the napkin she was playing with in her lap. "Many times, I feel so out of place here. I feel that people are staring at me."

"Well, they probably are!" Nora said. "But it's only because you're so pretty."

"That's not it," Moni said. "I think they are secretly laughing at my clothes. I do not dress like people here. I look different, funny."

Nora clicked her tongue, exasperated. "You're a *trendsetter*, Moni. People here just haven't caught up with the latest fashions yet." She gestured at Moni's jumper. "Just you wait — in two months, all the stores in the mall will probably be filled with brown corduroy mini-jumpers."

Moni looked up into Nora's kind, concerned eyes and suddenly she knew the time was right to confess everything, starting with the fact that the jumper was eight years old. She took a deep breath. "Nora, this jumper was made —"

"What will you girls have?" the waitress interrupted, her pen poised above an order pad.

Moni immediately ordered a hot fudge sundae, but it took a few minutes for Nora to decide between frozen yogurt and carrot cake. She finally chose the carrot cake and some herb tea.

"Now, what were we talking about?" Nora asked.

"Nothing," Moni said, having once again lost her nerve.

Over at Lucy's grandmother's house, Jennifer dangled a piece of fish over Dazzle's head. The Siamese cat took a swipe at it with his left paw.

"That's ten out of ten," Jen said, marking it down on her chart with one hand and allowing Dazzle to eat the fish with the other. "Dazzle is definitely left-pawed."

Mrs. Armanson got up from her chair, chuckling. "I'm not surprised. Not after he's lived with an old lefty like me for nine years. Would you girls like some mineral water?"

Jennifer stared at her, wide-eyed. "What did you just say, Mrs. Armanson?"

"I asked if you girls wanted some mineral water. I have some Calistoga — "

"No, no, I mean about you and Dazzle both being left-handed," Jennifer interrupted in her excitement. "That's what you said, didn't you?"

Mrs. Armanson nodded with a puzzled expression.

"May I use your phone?" Jennifer asked, jumping up from the floor.

Mrs. Armanson pointed to it on a little table on the other side of the living room. "There's a phone book on that shelf underneath it, if you need it."

Jennifer flipped eagerly through the phone book and found the number of Mr. Rochester, her English teacher. He answered on the second ring. "Mr. Rochester, your Edna is left-pawed. What are you?" Jen asked breathlessly.

"I'm left-handed, too," the teacher said.

Jennifer nodded to herself and said good-bye after promising to explain her question before English the next day.

She next called Mrs. Parsons, who lived across the street from the Manns. Mrs. Parsons, she found out, was right-handed, just like Slinky. Then Jen called Steve Crowley to make sure he was right-handed like Furperson. He was!

Across the room, Mrs. Armanson and Denise laughed each time they heard Jennifer shout with delight. As she hung up with Steve, Jennifer suddenly realized that she was being rude by making all these phone calls when she should be visiting with Mrs. Armanson. After all, she could confirm the rest of the cases on her own phone when she got home.

But Jen couldn't talk about anything else. She skipped over to Mrs. Armanson and grabbed the woman's hands. "Thank you, thank you, thank you! You've saved my life . . . or at least my science project." She giggled.

"Now how did I do that?"

"It's kind of a complicated story, but my hypothesis was that cats are ambidextrous. I found out that that's generally not true. I can't just leave it at that, though. That conclusion doesn't shed any light on the subject or break any new ground. But when you made that comment about you and Dazzle . . . well, suddenly the pieces sort of fit together. And now I think I've come to a terrific conclusion: Cats use the same 'hand' as their owners do!"

"But you told me that all the cats at the animal shelter are ambidextrous," Denise said.

Jennifer jumped up and down. "But don't you see, Denise? They're ambidextrous because they don't have owners!"

Denise nodded thoughtfully. "I bow to you, Dr. Einstein."

Jennifer grinned, twirled around in a

circle, snapped her fingers, and let loose a very unscientific "aww-right!"

To Jennifer's surprise, Nora called her that night. I guess she doesn't consider what happened between us this afternoon to have been a fight, Jennifer thought, relieved, when she heard Nora's "*Allô!*" The French greeting, however, annoyed Jen. It reminded her of Moni and how she hadn't wanted Jen to go along to Temptations.

"Is Moni still there?" Jennifer asked stiffly.

Nora yawned. "Uh-uh. My mom just drove her home. We came up with a relatively edible verson of last night's Zucchini Bread Squares. But the recipe still needs a little work. So what's happening with you?"

In a cool tone of voice, Jennifer described how she'd come up with the new conclusion for her science project.

"Oh, Jen, that's *splendide!*" Nora cried. "Why didn't you call and let me know the second you got home?"

Nora's second use of a French word just further irritated Jennifer. "Because I knew you'd be busy with your *best friend,*" she burst out.

Nora drew in her breath with surprise. "Oh, Jen, she's not my best friend. You are, and you know it."

"No, I *don't* know it! All I ever hear from you anymore is Moni this and Moni that. And you never have time to do anything with *me* anymore. You're always with her!"

"Jennifer, we're only talking about two nights. *Just two nights.* Tonight and last night."

"And this afternoon," Jennifer said.

Nora sighed. "I just can't believe what I'm hearing. Jennifer Mann, champion of animals, champion of the homeless, champion of senior citizens, the person who once confessed she'd like to take care of everyone in the entire world, is on my case just for being nice to a lonely new girl." She stopped. "Hey, wait a minute, doesn't this conversation sound familiar? Seems to me you got pretty angry at me not too long ago because I resented it when *you* befriended a new girl . . . Denise! I still remember what you said: 'Have a heart, Nora. She's lonely and misses her old friends and her old home and she doesn't feel like she fits in here at all.' Sounds just like Moni, too, doesn't it? *So have a heart, Jennifer!*"

"But when —"

"I admit it," Nora interrupted, "I was jealous at first when you started hanging around Denise back then. But remember how I ended up handling it? I just let it be! *I* realized that our friendship is so strong that other people can't hurt it."

"Oh, yeah? Well, I know a certain French girl who's trying her very hardest to do just that. The Denise thing was entirely different. At least *she* never tried to keep me away from you, which Moni is obviously — "

"I'll say the Denise thing was entirely different," Nora interrupted again. "She came to Cedar Groves to stay! She's not here for only a few measly months like Moni is. So I had much more reason to worry about you and Denise than you do to worry about me and Moni!"

"You just can't think straight or see the truth when it comes to Moni, can you?" Jennifer snapped. "You already proved that at lunch today when you shot down Denise just for trying to help us see that Moni — "

"I'm not going to listen to you insult Moni," Nora said. "Good-bye." She hung up.

Jennifer stared at the receiver in her hand, unable to believe Nora had hung up on her. "This is all her fault," Jennifer whispered. "She's being pigheaded and mean and thoughtless, and she owes me an apology."

At the Ryans', Nora rolled away from the telephone on her nightstand. "This is all her fault," Nora said aloud. "She's being petty, jealous, and paranoid, and she owes me an apology."

Each may have been convinced that the other was wrong. But each also fell asleep crying.

Chapter 12

The next morning, Tommy and Mitch waited impatiently on the school's front steps for Steve to arrive with the Jason pictures.

Mitch shaded his eyes from the early-morning sunlight and peered down the street. "I think I see Steve coming . . . yeah, that's him."

He and Tommy were so eager to see the pictures that they left the steps and jogged to meet Steve halfway down the block.

Steve was grinning widely. "I deserve a medal for these, if I do say so myself," he said, pulling a sheet of paper from his binder and handing it to Tommy. He had mounted two pictures on it. The first featured Nora, looking very peeved, swatting at Jason with a blurry hand. Jason's mouth was hanging open, with one of his fingers, dripping yogurt, on the way to it.

Tommy and Mitch hooted. "Look at that

goofy expression on his face!" Tommy said. "Duh?"

The other photo was a close-up of Jason wearing pencils in his nose.

Mitch and Tommy doubled over with laughter.

"He looks like some kind of pygmy warrior," Mitch said.

"Or a reject elephant," Steve said, joining in the laughter.

Underneath the pictures, Steve had printed "THE REAL JASON ANTHONY" in large letters with a red crayon.

"So how are we going to get this to Moni?" Steve asked. "Maybe you should give it to her, Ryder. You seem to have the most luck with women."

"Not with that one," Tommy said, shaking his head. "She won't let me near her. Yet. This little document may change all that, though." He rattled the paper on which the pictures were mounted. "For now, it's probably better if we get this to her anonymously."

"We could just stick it in her locker over at the high school," Steve said.

"Yeah," Tommy said. "Who volunteers?"

"Not me," Steve said. "I took the pictures and got them developed."

"And I was the one who 'borrowed' Jason's skateboard," Tommy said. "Mitch, you're elected. It's time you did your share in solving the 'Why Jason?' mystery."

Mitch shrugged out of his letter sweater and tied it around his waist. "But I don't even know where her locker is. Do you?"

Tommy and Steve shook their heads. "Just go over to the locker corridor at the high school and ask any guy," Steve said. I'm sure they all know where Moni Gorgeous's locker is."

Mitch nodded and headed for the high school.

Meanwhile, Jason was already in the high school locker corridor, trying to wedge his poem into Moni's locker. He had it three-quarters of the way in when it stuck. Darn! He had folded it too small and it was too thick. And now he couldn't pull it out or push it in. Jason glanced down the hall, afraid he'd see Moni coming. Instead he saw Mitch, though Mitch was looking around himself, seemingly lost, and hadn't yet spotted Jason. What was Mitch doing in the high school?

But all of a sudden, Jason panicked. Hey, he couldn't let Mitch see him at Moni's locker! If the guys ever got ahold of one of his Moni poems, Mitch would have eyewitness proof that it really *was* Jason writing them and putting them in Moni's locker. Jason wouldn't be able to claim it was some other guy doing it just as a gag, as he had always figured he'd be able to. He paled at the thought of the guys ribbing him about this latest disgustingly mushy poem. They might even call him "Rosy Fair" straight through till he graduated from high school!

On a flash of inspiration, Jason scooted across the corridor and found his brother Ed's locker — number 623. He leaned against it, relieved. Now, if Mitch asked him what he was doing in the high school locker corridor, he had a perfectly good excuse: Ed had forgotten his lunch money and Mom had asked Jason to bring it to him.

Mitch finally spotted Jason slouched against the locker. He had to restrain himself from laughing aloud with sheer joy at his luck. Jason was obviously waiting for Moni at her locker. Now Mitch wouldn't even have to ask anybody where it was! Jason, the poor dumb jerk, was actually playing a helpful role in the plan to expose him as a poor dumb jerk! All Mitch had to do was to wait for Moni to get to her locker and for the two of them to leave.

Pretending that he didn't see Jason, Mitch ambled past him with a casual air. He turned down another corridor but stopped short as soon as he was around the corner. Peeking around it, he could still see Jason leaning against the locker, though the corridor was quickly filling up. Luckily, Jason, with his red hair, easily stood out in the crowd. Mitch leaned against the wall and waited.

When Mitch had walked by Jason, Jason had had a sudden spark of suspicion: Maybe Mitch had come to the high school to deliver the pictures to Moni. But Jason quickly rejected that idea. In the first place, Mitch wasn't carrying pictures, he was carrying a piece of paper. And in the second place, it would be more cruel — and therefore more *likely* — for the guys to spring the pictures on Moni when Jason was there to witness her reaction. In biology, say. Or maybe in the cafeteria at lunch. Jason shuddered a little in anticipation of that unhappy event . . . and crossed his fingers that the poem would lessen the damage the pictures were bound to do.

Thinking about the poem, Jason looked across the corridor to where he could see it sticking out a little from Moni's locker. He was anxious to get back across the corridor and finish pushing it all the way in. But Mitch had to come back this way . . . and what if he did so just as Jason was pushing in the poem? No, Jason thought with a sigh, he'd just have to wait until after Mitch came by again.

And he fervently hoped Mitch would do so very soon. Jason knew Moni never went into the high school in the morning until right before the bell, but it was getting dangerously close to that right now. He went cold again — this time at the thought of being present when Moni read the poem. What if it made her so happy she'd try to kiss him? Or what if she asked him to read it aloud? He'd probably start laughing like a maniac or — worse — everyone within hearing distance would. Or he'd do some other totally uncool thing so that the poem would make things even more awful for him today, not better.

"Come on, Mitch, come on!" he muttered aloud.

Around the corner, Mitch was wishing just as hard that Moni would get to her locker so that she and Jason would leave the corridor. Mitch had already been late to homeroom once this month and, if it happened again, he'd be forced to sit out the first quarter of the next home game.

Finally, when only two minutes remained before the bell, Jason decided he could no longer afford either to wait for

Mitch or to try to get the poem farther into the locker. The risk of encountering Moni was too great. He left his brother's locker, glancing across the corridor at Moni's. Jason was pretty sure no one would come along and try to pull the poem out. Even if someone did try, it probably wouldn't come out since it was wedged in there so tightly. Moni herself would probably have to open her locker in order to extract the paper. Jason got on his skateboard and jetted down the walkway toward the junior high, keeping his eyes carefully peeled for a French girl with black hair.

Mitch breathed a sigh of relief when he saw Jason give up waiting for Moni. He loped down the corridor and carefully inserted the paper with the pictures on it into locker number 623. Then he ran for his homeroom.

Thirty seconds later, Jason's brother Ed approached his locker and twirled the combination lock. He saw the pictures the instant he opened the door. Taking the paper in his hand for a closer inspection, he shook his head, grinning.

"Someone wasted a lot of time and effort trying to convince me of something I've known for thirteen years," he said with a snort. Ed tossed "THE REAL JASON ANTHONY" into a trash can on his way to homeroom.

Dressing for school that morning, Jennifer had decided not to speak to Nora until Nora said she was sorry. Dawdling over a granola breakfast at the Ryans', Nora had made the same decision regarding Jennifer. Both girls dreaded being near each other either alone or in the crowd under such conditions. Each had timed it so that she'd get to school just before the bell rang and not have to hang out with everybody else on the steps.

So Jen and Nora both found themselves, to their dismay, hurrying up the school's deserted front steps at the same time. Why did they have to think alike, Jen thought bitterly, even when they were fighting? Each pretended not to see the other. Nora, going through the school door a few seconds before Jennifer, didn't bother to hold it open for Jen.

With Nora a few strides ahead, the girls marched in frozen silence down the main corridor, which was now almost empty. Each stopped at her locker, removed her jacket, and got her English textbook. Then the girls continued on toward their homeroom, this time with Jennifer in the lead.

Between each of the morning's classes,

each girl walked with other people. But that wasn't entirely out of the ordinary, so nobody thought to ask either one if something was wrong.

During PE, however, Susan Hillard got suspicious when Jennifer and Nora did their aerobics on opposite sides of the drafty gym. After class, Susan approached Nora as she was changing out of her gym clothes.

Susan gestured toward Jennifer, who was dressed and on her way out of the locker room. "Having a little tiff are we?" Susan said sweetly with one of her famous nasty smiles.

"None of your business," Nora said.

"Oh, so we *are* having a little tiff. Well, then, let's hear all the gory details."

Nora frowned at her. "What is your problem, Susan? Do you enjoy it when other people are unhappy?"

"Not particularly. It's just that an occasional fight adds — how you say? — well . . . *spice.* An occasional fight adds spice to a typical dull day here at Cedar Groves Junior High. Especially when it's between our famous best-friends-since-kindergarten duo."

"That's where you belong with that attitude, Susan," Nora snapped. "Kindergarten."

"A weak put-down, Nora. Very."

But it was the best she could do when

she was feeling so miserable, Nora thought, slamming her gym locker door and flouncing away.

At noon, both Jennifer and Nora sat at their usual table in the cafeteria. But Jennifer sat next to Denise and pretended to be completely and totally engrossed in hearing about what Denise and Timothy Marks had talked about on the phone the night before. Similarly, Nora seemed just as intent on hearing Lucy's blow-by-blow description of a movie her dad had rented at the video store. In this way, neither girl had any reason to look at or speak to the other.

"Something feels *different* about the atmosphere at this table today," Susan announced at one point, her eyes wide with innocence. "But I just can't put my finger on it. Whatever could it be?"

By that time, the other girls at the table suspected that there was something wrong between Nora and Jennifer. But none of them wanted to make the situation even more uncomfortable for the two girls. Susan's comment was ignored.

Moni came in a few minutes after lunch had started. She scanned the cafeteria for Jason and then sat down beside Nora. "Do not tell anyone," she whispered in Nora's ear, "but Jason has written me another love poem!"

Nora nearly choked on a bite of apple.

"He left biology so fast that I could not tell him how much I liked it," Moni continued to whisper. "I was hoping he would be here now, but he is not. Oh, where is that boy?"

He was out on the school's front steps, eating his sack lunch and freezing.

The boys obviously hadn't given Moni the pictures yet, he figured. After all, Moni had stared at him lovingly — no doubt because of the poem — as he rushed in and out of biology. Nope, those creeps were obviously planning to lay the pictures on Moni when there was the largest possible audience to witness his humiliation. And where was that? In the cafeteria, of course! Well, he wasn't going to be there. At least *that* part of the boys' little plan was spoiled.

"Jason," he said aloud, "you're just too smart for them."

But if he was so much smarter, Jason asked himself, shivering, why was he the one out here freezing to death?

In the cafeteria, Tommy, Mitch, and Steve were watching when Moni sat down next to Nora and whispered in her ear.

"So she finally went to her locker and saw the pictures," Tommy said, relieved.

"I bet she's getting on Nora's case for not warning her from the start that Jason is geek time. Nice work, guys." He shook Mitch's hand, then Steve's.

"I just hope I'm around when Mademoiselle Gorgée confronts Monsieur Anthony with the evidence," Steve said with a laugh. "What is the French word for 'disgusting'?"

Tommy laughed, too. "Or 'weird'? Or 'revolting'? Let's look them up in Armand's French dictionary next period so we'll know what she's shouting at Jason if she finds herself at a loss for English words!"

After school that day, Jason jerked on his Sony Walkman and zoomed down the main corridor on his skateboard, knowing that unless he was off the school grounds within the next thirty seconds he was sure to face the dreaded confrontation with Moni. Would she be disgusted because of the pictures? Or sweet and forgiving because of the poem? Or a little of each? Or more disgusted than forgiving? That was probably it. But he wasn't going to stick around to find out.

He was within seconds of the main doors when he heard her calling his name.

"Jason! Jason!" Moni shouted. "I need to talk to you about what I got this morning!"

Tommy and Mitch, at Tommy's locker, grinned at each other. "All right!" Tommy said, slapping Mitch's outstretched palms. "She's gonna shout what she thinks about Jason and his lovely pictures for all the world to hear!"

"Jason, stop! I must speak to you! It was . . . *magnifique!*"

So the pictures had had no effect, Jason thought as he kept on moving. Or else the poem was even more powerful than he'd realized!

Mitch and Tommy stared at each other, their mouths hanging open in shock, unable to believe that they'd really heard what they'd heard.

"Conclusion," Tommy said, "Moni *doesn't care* that he's really a jerk." He shook his head.

"Jason!" shouted Moni. "It was *magnifique. You* are *magnifique!*"

"And you, Moni Gorgeous," muttered Mitch, "are *weird.*"

Chapter 13

Thursday and Friday of that week were almost exact reruns of Wednesday— which made them among the most miserable days Nora and Jennifer had ever known. In the evenings, they moped around their houses and their phones remained suspiciously silent. It was obvious to the families of both that the girls had quarreled. But neither family said anything, afraid that interfering might make things worse.

Jeff hasn't hollered at me, Eric walks by my bedroom door on tiptoe, and Dad brought home a red carnation for me, Jennifer wrote in her diary on Thursday night. *They're treating me as if I were sick or something — like I have the flu or chickenpox. I wish that were the problem.*

The only good thing about Friday for Jennifer was that she came up with an idea that would not only help Cedar

Groves' homeless cat population, it would also distract her from her misery about Nora. She went to school early to discuss it with Mr. Morris, the biology teacher.

At the beginning of biology that day, Mr. Morris told the class that Jennifer had an announcement to make.

She stood up, blushing a little. "I think some of you know that I'm a volunteer at the Cedar Groves Animal Shelter every Saturday afternoon," Jen said, her voice quavering a little. She cleared her throat, and her voice got stronger: "All the cats live in one room at the shelter — it's known as the Cat Room. All the cats, that is, except for the one or two who enjoy picking fights." There was scattered laughter. "They have private apartments. Anyway, the Cat Room is very nice. It's got toys, scratching posts, and lots of little nooks and crannies for the cats to curl up in. But it's not outdoors, and we all know how much cats like to go outside at times."

Charlie Parker let loose a pathetic yowl, as if he were waiting at a door to be let out. The class laughed.

Jennifer smiled. "Of course, it would be dangerous to just let the shelter cats loose outdoors. They might get lost or run over. So the people at the shelter want to do the next best thing. They want to build a screened-in porch for the cats. It'll be connected to the Cat Room via one of those little doggy doors, so that the cats can go in and out whenever they feel like it. Doesn't that sound like a nice thing to do for poor homeless animals that nobody wants?"

She looked so earnest and sad that no one in the class had the heart to argue or make a smart remark. Several people nodded at her.

"That's what I thought you'd think!" Jennifer said happily. "And that's why I'm organizing a bake sale to be held in conjunction with next Saturday's Fifteenth Annual Cedar Groves Junior High Science Fair. All proceeds will go to the Cedar Groves Animal Shelter Cat Porch Fund. See, the porch can't be built without community contributions."

Tears stung Nora's eyes. It was the kind of project that Jen was famous for. The kind of project that, in the past, always made Nora groan, "Oh, Jen, you and your causes!" The kind of project that Nora, each time with growing enthusiasm, always ended up helping Jennifer plan and pull off. Jennifer hadn't even mentioned this one to Nora. And that was scary. Maybe their friendship wasn't just temporarily off . . . maybe Jennifer considered the breakup permanent! With a sharp pang of jealousy, Nora glanced over at Denise.

Maybe Jennifer had planned the project with *her*.

"I'll take care of providing the tables to display the stuff, and I'll also be the cashier on the day of the sale," Jennifer continued. "All you guys have to do is supply the baked goodies. I have a sign-up sheet here."

Jennifer held up a piece of notebook paper on which she had printed the words NAME and BRINGING. In large letters, Jennifer had also filled in her own name and BROWNIES under the respective categories. Nora was relieved to see that Denise hadn't yet volunteered to bring anything. That meant she wasn't helping Jennifer with the project. Yet.

Jennifer tacked the sign-up sheet to a corner of Mr. Morris's front bulletin board. "Please sign up as soon as possible," she said. "By Monday at the latest."

At Temptations after school that day, Tommy, Mitch, Steve, and Andy drowned their sorrows in hot fudge.

"Twice today, Moni Gorgeous cut me dead when I tried to talk to her," Tommy said with a sigh. "Once before school, when she was trying to catch up with Jason, and once right after biology."

"And she said '*Ta bouche!*' to me when I whistled at her after French," Mitch said, his expression glum. "I asked Armand what that meant and guess what? It means 'shut up!' "

Tommy nodded sympathetically. "I hate to admit it, guys, but I, for one, am about ready to give up on her. She's impossible. Anybody want to throw out a final hypothesis as to how she could possibly prefer you-know-who over the rest of us?"

Steve yawned. "Hypothesis: Maybe she needs glasses."

The others laughed.

"Hypothesis," said Mitch, "maybe she actually likes the way he looks."

The others laughed even harder.

"Hypothesis," said Andy, "maybe he's paying her to act crazy about him — just to impress us."

"He'd have to be a millionaire to pay her enough to do that!" Mitch cried, pounding a fist on the table.

"Wait — I've got another one," Steve said. "Hypothesis: Maybe Moni's really after Jason's brother Ed. Maybe she's just using Jason to get to Ed."

There was silence as the boys mulled this over.

"Nah," Mitch finally said.

"I agree with Mitch," Tommy said thoughtfully. "Moni's obviously not the calculating type — she's the aggressive type. When she wants something, she goes after it. Directly."

"*It* is the word," Steve said, laughing.

"Andy!" Mia Stevens was standing in the doorway, waving for Andy to join her. She was wearing what looked to be a plastic garbage bag belted at the waist. Her hair was done up in bright lime-green spikes and the area between her eyes and eyebrows sported painted-on tiger stripes.

Andy got up. "I'm sticking with Mia," he said. "*She*, at least, is easy to figure out."

The other guys waited until he'd left the table before completely cracking up.

Chapter 14

On Saturday morning, Jennifer and Nora unknowingly arrived at the Twin Rivers Mall within five minutes of each other. Denise's mother let Denise and Jennifer out at one end of the mall while Nora's father dropped off Nora and Moni at the other.

As it turned out, neither Nora nor Jen had as good a time as they usually did when they went to the mall together.

The problem with shopping with Denise was that she had her mother's charge card and a note giving her permission to use it. And did she ever use it! If Denise liked something, she didn't have to spend any time debating whether her budget could handle it, whether it would go with anything she had, or whether she could get it cheaper at another mall store. She simply bought it. Jennifer usually found shopping with Denise a deflating experience . . .

especially if she herself craved an accessory, pair of shoes, or outfit that Denise was buying.

"Oh, Jen, you should get one of these blouses, too," Denise said as she herself did so at the sales counter in Steven's. "You'd look even better in it. Brunettes always look the best in red."

"I only have eleven dollars," Jennifer said, biting her tongue to keep from adding that this was the third time she'd had to remind Denise of that fact.

Meanwhile, Nora had led Moni in and out of the Sly Fox, Bradley's, and a couple of other stores. When they got to Steven's, about ten minutes after Denise and Jennifer had left, Nora took a blouse off a front rack and handed it to Moni. It was identical to the blouse Denise had purchased.

"This would look gorgeous on you with your dark hair," Nora said. "Try it on."

"But I didn't bring any money," Moni said, neglecting to add, of course, that she hadn't had any money to bring.

"You don't have to buy it," Nora said. "Don't you just want to try it on?"

Moni looked at Nora as if she were crazy. "Why? If I am not going to buy it?"

"Just for the fun of it, I guess," Nora said sheepishly. She had never really thought about it before. "Or so you know what you look good in when you *do* have the money."

Moni continued to look skeptical. "Wouldn't they get mad?" She gestured toward the sales clerks at the counter.

"They *expect* people to try stuff on," Nora said.

"Even when the person doesn't have the money for it?"

"Moni, they don't have X-ray eyes. They can't see inside your wallet. They also can't read your mind. Look, after you try this on, if someone asks you why you're not buying it, you can just say it's too big or something. But no one will ask. Jen and I have tried things on in here a million times, and no one's ever said a word, whether we ended up buying or not."

Moni hung the blouse back on the rack. "No, thanks. I do not feel like trying it on."

Nora took Moni to a few other stores, but it became more and more obvious that the French girl wasn't really looking at things. She was just sort of following Nora around.

"Don't you like shopping, Moni?" Nora finally asked.

"I love it. When do we begin?"

It was Nora's turn to look at Moni as if she were crazy. "We *are* shopping."

"But you haven't bought anything.

When you suggested we go shopping, I thought that you needed to buy something and that I would help you pick it out."

"Moni, I couldn't buy anything even if I wanted to. I only have five dollars, and I'm saving that to treat us to a snack. See, in America — well, at least to Jen and me — 'going shopping' doesn't necessarily mean going to buy something. It mostly means just hanging out at the mall, looking at stuff, and maybe trying it on. Don't you think it's fun to just look?"

"I guess so," Moni said.

But Nora could tell that Moni didn't mean it. She sighed. "Come on. I think it's time for that snack."

Nora led Moni down the wing of the mall that was lined mostly with restaurants and fast-food places.

"Want to get a Coke at Sluggo's?" Nora asked, pointing at a hot dog counter.

"Oh, look at that little place!" Moni said, pointing in the opposite direction. "It is called 'Boulangerie et Livres!' That is French for 'Bakery and Books.' Let's go there."

Nora hesitated. The little coffee shop and bookstore that had opened just recently had become sort of special to her and Jennifer. It was the kind of place where customers sipped coffee at tiny tables and discussed famous authors with each other as if they'd had dinner with the authors the night before.

Jennifer and Nora had always felt one hundred percent more sophisticated than usual the second they walked through the door of the place. They'd sit at a dime-sized table and order coffee, even though both hated coffee, because to order any other beverage seemed like an incredibly childish thing to do in that atmosphere. The girls also had an unspoken rule that they couldn't say anything to each other in Boulangerie et Livres unless it had to do with books — and it had better be about *classic* books, thank you. So they'd make polite chitchat about *Little Women* and *Wuthering Heights* while blowing on their coffee — usually till it was ice cold. Then they'd force themselves to down it, trying to hide their "yuck!" expressions from other patrons. Either Nora or Jen always ended up breaking the "books only" rule to whisper, "Why can't coffee taste as good as it smells?"

The memories filled Nora with sadness. "Not here, Moni . . . "

But the French girl was already pulling her through the café's doors. They sat down at a table right next to a display case full of French pastries and breads. When the waitress came, both girls ordered croissants. Nora ordered decaffeinated coffee and Moni asked for *café crème*. Of course, Nora thought, coffee with lots of cream was *so* French.

The waitress brought their order right away.

Nora giggled and tore off a bit of croissant. "Jen would die if she saw me eating one of these," she said. "I mean, I'm always lecturing her about how they're filled with butter and dangerously high in cholesterol. But how could I resist with them staring me in the face like that?" She nodded toward the display case.

Moni took a sip of her drink, then dabbed at her mouth with a napkin. "I know you and Jennifer have had an argument, but I do not know the reason and I do not like to pry."

"Oh, Moni, the other night we just — " Nora stopped. How could she tell the French girl that the fight was over *her*?

Moni waved a hand. "It is all right. It is none of my business. I only brought it up because I wanted to say that I think you must miss her terribly. You mention her a lot."

Nora nodded miserably and felt the pressure of tears behind her eyes. "How are you and Jason doing?" she asked quickly, hoping a new subject would prevent her from crying.

Moni sighed. "Well, he writes beautiful poetry for me, but we almost never speak. He is always so busy. It is frustrating, and yet the lack of personal contact I have with him has added to his — oh, how you say — *mystique*?"

Nora bit back a burst of laughter at the image of Jason as a dashing, mysterious figure. "Mystique is the same in English as it is in French. We probably stole it from you guys." She took a bite of croissant. "Mmm . . . aren't these *fantastique*?"

Moni eyed what was left of the croissant on her plate. "I know it will sound impossible, but the croissants my father bakes . . . I mean, the ones that are baked in his bakeries . . . they are even lighter and flakier than these."

"I keep forgetting that your dad owns a big chain of — " Nora stopped suddenly and caught her breath. Jennifer and Denise had just come through the door. Oh, Jen, Nora thought, how can you be so disloyal as to bring Denise *here*?

She had no idea that Jennifer, who had spotted Nora at the same instant, was thinking the exact same thing about Nora being there with Moni. Nora was also unaware that it had been Denise's choice to come here, just as it had been Moni's.

"This place reminds me of a Swiss café in the Alps my friends and I would sometimes go to after skiing," Denise had said, pulling Jennifer inside.

"Oh, Denise, I can't eat here," Jennifer said as they stood in the doorway.

Denise followed Jennifer's dismayed eyes to Nora across the room. Denise tossed her hair over her shoulder and headed for a table. "We have as much right to eat here as Nora and Boney Gulp do," she said over her shoulder. "Come on."

Not wanting to make a scene, Jennifer followed her. At the table, Jennifer ordered coffee — feeling, as usual, that to order the Coke she craved would be viewed as babyish in a place like Boulangerie et Livres. But Denise, with her usual supreme confidence, did just that. When the drinks came, Jennifer sat in silence and listened to Denise talk about clothes. She tried not to look over at Nora.

Meanwhile, Moni had not noticed the arrival of the two other girls. She stood up at the table she shared with Nora. "While you are finishing your croissant, do you mind if I look at the books?" she asked Nora.

Nora shook her head, and Moni went to the bookshelves in the back of the shop. With the French girl gone and no one to talk to, Nora found it almost impossible to keep her eyes away from Jennifer and Denise's table. She forced herself to read her paper placemat, on which was printed a biography of the Brontë sisters.

But finally, just after both Nora and Jen took their first sips of their now ice-cold coffees, their eyes met. Involuntarily, they grinned when they saw each other's "yuck!" expressions. Almost immediately, though, the grins were gone, replaced by icy glares. And then both girls were looking down into their laps to hide the sadness that had replaced the glares that had replaced that split second of the old warmth.

Just then, Moni returned to the table carrying a heavy green book entitled *The Greatest Poems of All Time*. "I certainly cannot buy this book today," she said, sitting down, "but I would like to look at it while we are here." She opened it to the table of contents. "Look, Nora," she said, pointing, "there is a whole chapter of poems about love. I bet they are not half as good as Jason's." She flipped to the page where that chapter started.

But Nora stood up abruptly. "I'm sorry, Moni, but I want to leave now," she said in a shaky voice, struggling not to cry. She left some money on the table and walked out of the store, not waiting for the French girl.

Reluctantly, Moni got up to follow Nora, first returning the book to the shelf. Unread.

Chapter 15

"I can't believe you people can be so heartless!" Jennifer nearly shouted at her biology class on Monday.

"Oh, Jennifer, it's not a matter of heart, it's a matter of *time*," Susan called out. "I, for one, do not have the time to bake something for your bake sale if I'm going to finish my science project in time."

There were several yells of, "Same here."

"Yeah, Jennifer, just because you finished your project doesn't mean everyone else has," Tommy said.

Jennifer stamped her foot. "I have *not* finished my project! I still have to put together my display. Even so, even if I have to stay up all night, I'm going to *make* time for those poor cats . . . those poor cats who are never petted or played with or even named. I'm — " Her voice broke, and she sat down quickly with her head down. Her hair hid her face.

Nora bit her lip and stared at Jen's bent head. When Nora had first walked into biology that morning and seen that the bake sale sign-up was still blank except for Jennifer's own name, she had been *glad.* It serves her right, Nora had thought.

But suddenly, Nora's heart broke for Jennifer. The events of the last week seemed trivial, the argument they'd had ridiculous, the way they'd both been acting silly. Waiting to see who would break down and say she was sorry first seemed incredibly childish. Suddenly, all that mattered was that this girl who cared so much for everybody, who could always be counted on to come through for everybody, was being totally let down by everybody.

Nora stood up. With her heels clacking in the utter silence, she marched to the bulletin board at the front of the room. In big block letters, she printed NORA RYAN and CARROT CAKE on the sign-up sheet. Then Nora turned around and faced the class, arms folded sternly across her chest. "Come on, you lazy people! Create a coffee cake for a cat! Bake banana bread for the babies! Choose cheesecake for charity! Make muffins matter!"

The class laughed, and Tracy and Susan trooped up to the front to add their names and contributions to the list. Nora finally allowed herself to look at Jennifer. Jen was grinning.

After class, they grabbed each other's hands in the hall and tried to talk at the same time.

"Oh, Nora, I'm sorry — "

"Oh, Jen, I'm sorry — "

"— I promise I won't let your friendship with Moni bother me . . . and I won't insult her . . . I just want you and me to — "

"— I promise I won't hang around with Moni so much . . . I mean, I would rather be with you anyway, and I'll do anything if you'll — "

"— See, now I think you were right, I think we *can* still be friends with other people, and it doesn't have to affect *our* friendship at all. In fact, I — "

"— I shouldn't have acted so snooty and know-it-all, like a — "

They stopped and laughed.

"Friends again?" Jen said simply.

"The best," Nora said.

They headed for their lockers, filling each other in about their lives for the past several days and exclaiming over how much they'd missed each other.

Jen twirled the combination of her lock and looked over at Nora shyly. "Last week, I kept wondering which one of us was going to break down and talk to the other first. Over the weekend, though, I started wondering if we'd ever speak to each other again."

Nora nodded, biting her lip. "Me, too. Especially after you gave me that dirty look in Boulangerie et Livres. You can really look mean when you want to, girl!"

"You should talk. I was just trying to look as mean as *you* did."

Nora laughed a little as she opened her locker. "Well, as it ends up, *I'm* the one who broke down first. If you can count my 'Make Muffins Matter' speech as breaking down. So I lose."

Jen shook her head and pointed at an envelope lying in the bottom of Nora's locker. Mystified, Nora opened it and took out a note:

Dear Nora,

I'm sorry for the things I said to you last week and for the way I've behaved. I will do anything to be friends again.

If you forgive me, please come over tonight. Jeff has cut the boards for our science projects, and we can work on our displays.

Love,
Jennifer

"I put that in your locker right before homeroom," Jen said. "So see? I broke down first. *I* lose."

Nora squeezed her hand. "How can we call it losing . . . when we both win?"

On the floor of the Manns' family room that evening, Nora covered her science project display boards with lemon-yellow burlap while Jennifer, with stencils, traced the letters ARE CATS AMBIDEXTROUS? onto black construction paper.

Jennifer seemed very quiet and glum to Nora — she said almost nothing and sighed a lot. Nora began to worry that she was having second thoughts about making up.

"Jen . . . are you mad at me?" Nora asked softly.

Jennifer looked up suddenly, and the sad, worried look in her eyes disappeared as she smiled. "Not anymore. I thought we settled that this morning."

"Then what's the matter?"

Jennifer sighed and threw down her pencil. "I'm going to have to cancel the Cat Porch Fund Bake Sale."

"Oh, Jen, no. Why?"

"Because only four of us offered to bring anything. That would make us a grand total of four bucks max."

"You wait — more people will volunteer to bring things," Nora said.

Jennifer shook her head. "I made today the deadline for signing up, remember? At first I figured some people were just too embarrassed to walk up there and sign up in front of the whole class like you and Susan and Tracy did. I thought they'd do it later, when no one was watching. But I went to Mr. Morris' classroom after school to check the list. . . . Nobody else signed it."

Nora clicked her tongue sympathetically.

Jennifer rubbed her eyes tiredly. "I really feel bad. You should have heard me bragging to Becky Barton, at the shelter, about how much our class would be donating to the fund."

For the second time that day, Nora couldn't bear to see her friend so sad. "Isn't there anything else we can do? Isn't there a bakery in town that might donate —" Suddenly, she leaped to her feet. "MONI!" she shouted. "Oh, Jennifer, Moni's dad would do it, I'm sure! Moni's dad would donate all the baked goods for our sale! What's one itty-bitty little junior high school bake sale to a multimillion-dollar bakery chain?"

She pulled Jennifer to her feet and tried to make Jennifer jump up and down with her in her excitement.

"Wait!" Jennifer said, pulling away.

"If you're so sure Moni's father would be willing to do this, why didn't Moni *herself* offer to ask him? How come she didn't mention the possibility in biology today?"

"Maybe she just didn't think of it," Nora said.

Jennifer raised an eyebrow skeptically.

Nora frowned for a minute, thinking, "Actually, she probably didn't offer because she thought people would think she was showing off," she finally said. "She really doesn't flaunt how rich she is. And Jen, she may act very cool and confident, but I happen to know that she really, deeply cares what people think of her."

It was Jennifer's turn to frown. "It's a great idea. But Nora, I just can't see myself asking her to do it. Not after all this stuff between you and me . . . I mean, it's pretty obvious she doesn't like me."

"I don't know why you think that, Jen. She's never said one word against you to me. In fact, she said something really sympathetic about how much we must have missed each other. But all of that's beside the point — because *I'll* be the one to ask her. I'm sure I can convince her." Nora danced toward the kitchen. "And I'm gonna do it right now!"

Jennifer tried to continue outlining the letters for her project as she overheard snatches of Nora's phone conversation with

Moni, but she was too nervous and excited.

After only about two minutes, she heard Nora hang up the phone and shout. The two girls crashed into each other as Jen ran for the kitchen and Nora for the family room.

"She says she's sure he'll do it!" Nora cried joyfully.

The girls joined hands and danced in a circle. After a minute, they collapsed, breathless, onto the floor.

"Oh, Jennifer," Nora panted, "just think how much more people will pay for fancy French petit fours and pastries than they ever would for Susan's lumpy old chocolate chip cookies or my *blah* carrot cake."

Jennifer smiled. "It'll all be thanks to you, Nora," she said warmly. "It was your idea. And you did the asking."

Nora hung her head. "It was the least I could do. It'll make up for my not being in on a project of yours from the start, like I always have been in the past." Nora looked up at Jennifer, eyes twinkling. "And that reminds me. Since I didn't get to groan it in the beginning, I'll groan it now—'Oh, Jen — you and your causes!' "

A half hour after Nora called her, Moni was still sitting, frozen in the same position, on her bed in the Bryants' house. The realization of what she had done kept flooding through her mind, pounding like a massive headache: She had promised that "Gorgée International" would fly in enough French pastries and breads to supply Jennifer's entire bake sale!

There was a sudden knock on the door, and Mrs. Bryant popped her head in. "Good-night, honey. Tom and I are— Moni! What's wrong?"

Moni tried to stretch her lips into a smile. "I'm just tired," she said hoarsely.

Mrs. Bryant stared at her, eyes narrowed with concern. "Are you sure that's all? Is there something you want to talk about, dear? You look so pale and . . . well, frightened."

I am terrified, Moni thought. "I am fine," she said.

When Mrs. Bryant finally closed the door, still looking skeptical, Moni fell back on the bed, her mind racing.

What on earth was she going to do?

One thing was for sure: There was absolutely no way she or her family could afford to donate all of that food, to say nothing about hiring a pilot and plane to fly it here! In fact, all of the spending money Moni had brought to last her entire stay in America wasn't enough to even buy an adequate number of cakes at the local Safeway.

Maybe she could say that her father refused to do it because he hated cats. Maybe she could say her father's employees had suddenly gone on strike. Maybe she could say the plane carrying the baked goods was grounded in New York because of bad weather. Maybe she should simply get on a plane herself tomorrow and return to France with no explanation. Maybe she should just confess everything.

Moni suddenly sobbed and covered her eyes as if the light in her room was unbearably bright. No matter what she did, she realized, she was going to be letting a whole bunch of people down. And they were going to hate her for it.

She rolled off the bed and got her purse from the closet. Taking out Jason's letter and the two poems, she laid them on her desk, smoothing out the folds. She reread them but could get no comfort from them. All she could think of was that, in the end, Jason would hate her, too. Jason would join the others in hating "the French *fraude*."

Moni closed her eyes tight, but the tears squeezed through them and fell on the well-worn sheets of paper with tiny plops.

What on earth was she going to do?

Chapter 16

Moni made herself sick . . . literally. When she woke up the next morning, after a long night of tossing and turning, her head was all stuffed up and her stomach queasy.

"Can people make themselves sick?" she asked Mrs. Bryant when the woman brought her a cup of hot tea with honey.

Mrs. Bryant felt Moni's forehead, her eyes full of worry. "Well, I'm no doctor . . . but I do think stress makes people more susceptible to catching things. It probably weakens the immune system. You're under a lot of stress right now, aren't you?"

Moni nodded and took a mouthful of hot tea, allowing it to trickle slowly down her sore throat.

"And there's nothing Tom and I can do to help?" Mrs. Bryant asked.

Not unless you can give me about a thousand dollars, Moni thought. "No, this is something I have to work out for myself," she said. "But thank you for your concern."

"Well, a few days of rest can only help," Mrs. Bryant said. "I'll call your school and tell them you'll be out."

So for the next three days — Tuesday, Wednesday, and Thursday — Moni stayed in bed. Awake, she coughed, blew her nose, worried, and cried a lot. Asleep, she had nightmares. In one, she was locked in a tiny room and couldn't get out. In another, a huge, shapeless, inhuman thing kept chasing her. And in the worst, she returned home and Maman and Papa threw her out of the house because they did not recognize her.

"But I am your daughter!" she kept crying.

"*These* are our daughters!" they shouted back, pointing at the twins, who acted like they, too, had never seen Moni before in their lives.

Nora called Moni after school each day, cheerful and full of news. The first afternoon, she informed Moni that vanilla had been the missing ingredient for making her Zucchini Bread Squares both nutritious *and* tasty — the perfect snack. The second day, Nora called to say that her sister Sally's boyfriend was borrowing a truck on Saturday morning to transport the baked goods from the airport to the school auditorium.

"What time should he be at the airport?" Nora asked.

"Um . . . eleven o'clock," Moni said, hating herself.

On Thursday, Nora called to offer Moni a ride with her and Jennifer to the science fair/bake sale, just two days away.

Moni's voice trembled. "But I cannot go — I did not do a project."

"You don't have to have done a project to go to the fair," Nora said. "The school wants the whole community to come — that's why it's on a Saturday."

"But — "

"And anyway, you *do* have a project: The bake sale! After all, if it weren't for you — "

"All right," Moni said, cutting her off.

What on earth was she going to do?

Thursday night, Nora and Jennifer went over to Steve Crowley's. For her science fair display, Jennifer needed Polaroid pictures of herself testing a cat. Nora had offered herself as the photographer; Steve had volunteered Furperson as the model.

After Furperson had once again demonstrated his right-paw tendencies with great dignity — even with the camera flashing in his face — Steve took the girls out to the garage to show them his own project: DOES EATING IN A RESTAURANT IMPROVE A PERSON'S MOOD? His display boards featured samples of questionnaires he had passed out to diners when they both entered and left his family's restaurant. A graph charted their responses by age.

Nora knelt down to read his conclusion.

"I haven't put the conclusion up yet," Steve said. "But the answer is that, except for children age six and under, going to a restaurant definitely improves a person's mood nine out of ten times in all other age groups."

Nora giggled. "Your dad must love it."

Steve nodded and laughed. "He's going to display the project in the restaurant for a whole month after the fair."

"I wonder what would have happened if you had come to the opposite conclusion," Jennifer said. "I mean, what would he have done if you'd found that eating in a restaurant puts most people in *bad* moods?"

"Oh, nothing," Steve said breezily. "He probably would have just fired me as his son."

"What did you find out about kids under six?" Nora asked.

"Going to a restaurant makes them crabby."

"Well, wasn't your dad upset about that?"

Steve winked at Nora. "Oh, no. See, they're not the ones with the big appetites and the credit cards."

Jennifer hopped up on a stool next to Mr. Crowley's workbench. "Well, it looks like everyone's going to finish their projects on time. All I needed for mine were these pictures, and Nora put the finishing touches on her display last night."

Steve sighed and shook his head. "All the projects are done except for the biggest one of all: WHY IS MONI GORGEOUS CRAZY ABOUT JASON ANTHONY, OF ALL PEOPLE?"

Nora laughed. "Oh, so somebody else has been wondering about that, too, huh?"

"Just me and a few hundred other guys."

"You spent a lot of time alone with her," Jennifer said to Nora. "How come you never just came right out and asked her?"

"I was afraid I wouldn't be able to keep from laughing," Nora said. Her expression turned serious. "Actually, I'm afraid this is going to remain one of the great mysteries of the world. Like how come animals get real restless right before an earthquake."

Jennifer's eyes sparkled. "Or why hot dogs come ten to a package but buns come only in eights."

"Either of those is easier to figure out than the Jason thing," Steve grumbled.

On Friday morning, though she was still sniffling, Moni forced herself to get up, get dressed, and go to school. She would absolutely have to tell Jennifer and Nora the truth today, while there was still time for them to cancel the bake sale. She would tell them right before biology.

Moni walked around school in a daze, hardly noticing when people said hello, hardly hearing a single word her teachers said. She was in such a daze of worry and fear and despair that she didn't even notice Jason when he rushed into biology, almost late, as usual. But today, so were Jennifer and Nora, for some reason. They came in just as the bell rang and Mr. Morris clapped to settle everyone down.

Mr. Morris droned on and on and on while Moni's anxiety mounted: She would have to tell Jennifer and Nora next period at lunch, perhaps in front of everyone!

Finally, about five minutes before the bell, Mr. Morris closed his textbook. "Jennifer has an announcement to make."

Jennifer stood up with a smile. "I just want everyone to know that if tomorrow's bake sale turns out to be a raging success, it will mostly be thanks to Moni Gorgée," she said. "The Gorgée family's baking corporation is donating *all* of the baked goods that will be for sale, with proceeds going to the Cedar Groves Animal Shelter Cat Porch Fund."

"What some people will do to get attention!" Denise whispered to Susan and Tracy, who sat near her. "I just hope Boney Gulp's baked goods are fresher than some of her other offerings have been — such as bell-bottoms!"

"I don't know about you," Jennifer was saying to the class, "but I think Moni deserves a hand!"

And then everybody — except Denise — got up and started clapping. Moni took one look around the room at their friendly, smiling faces . . . and couldn't bear the sight. She would never, ever be able to tell Jen and Nora the truth now! With a shaky and fake smile, she stumbled across the room toward the door, mumbling "I have been sick," to Mr. Morris as she passed him. And then she ran down the hall to the girls' restroom, threw herself against the door, and collapsed on the floor inside, tears streaming down her face as loud sobs racked her body.

Nora and Jennifer found her there, only a minute later, crying hysterically.

"Moni, what's the matter?" Nora said, taking her by the shoulders and shaking her gently.

"Je ne sais pas à quel saint me vouer," Moni sobbed.

"Speak English, Moni," Nora cried. "We can't understand you!"

"Quelle salade!" Moni said, burying her face in her hands and crying noisily.

Jennifer grabbed Nora's arm and pulled her away from the French girl. "I think she's too upset to remember any English, Nora."

Nora rung her hands. "What should we do? I'm scared."

Jennifer covered her eyes for a minute, thinking. "I know . . . let's get Denise! She speaks French as well as she speaks English."

"Oh, Jen, no . . . not Denise. You know how she feels about —" Nora broke off, afraid that Moni was listening. But Moni was taking great, loud gulps of air, oblivious.

"We don't have any other choice," Jennifer said. "Except Mr. Armand. And he can't come in here."

Nora nodded, frowning, and Jennifer flew out of the restroom to get Denise from the cafeteria. She was back within two minutes, the blonde girl in tow. Denise looked annoyed when she came through the door, but her expression softened as she took in the way Moni was huddled against the wall, sobbing pitifully, her black hair wild and tangled.

Denise crouched down next to the girl. "Moni. what's the matter? *Qu'est-ce qu'il y a?*" she asked in a gentle tone.

Moni looked up at her, red eyes wide with surprise. She was silent for several seconds. Then a torrent of French suddenly burst from her lips and the tears began to fall again.

Denise bit her lip and stood up. "I think it would be better if you guys left," she said to Jen and Nora. "Don't worry, I'll take care of this." She ended up having to push the girls, protesting every step of the way, out the door. Then she sat down next to Moni underneath the paper towel dispenser on the cold tile floor. And for the next half-hour she listened as Moni — in a halting voice, punctuated with sobs, and totally in French — told the whole story, from Cameron Carson's arrival in Fleur to Moni's arrival in Cedar Groves.

When Moni finished, she dropped her head to her drawn-up knees and the room was utterly silent.

"Oh, Moni, you poor girl," Denise finally said. "I never would have guessed."

Moni's head shot up. "You mean, you did not suspect something like this all along?"

"Not at all."

"But, you never liked me — "

"Because I thought you were a snob, and I hate snobs," Denise said. "But now I see that what I thought was snobby was just plain *scared*. I'm sorry I misjudged you, Moni."

Moni was shaking her head in disbelief. "I cannot believe it. I cannot believe you are not shouting at me in anger, hating me for being such a fraud."

"Listen, I can't exactly congratulate you on what you've done, but I can certainly understand it. I guess nobody ever told you that just a few short months ago, Jennifer and Nora found another girl crying in this very same bathroom, another girl who was terrified she would never fit in at an American school." Denise's smile was sad.

Moni gasped. "*You?*"

Denise nodded. "But the one thing I had going for me that you didn't was that I knew all Americans weren't creeps like your Cameron Carson." Denise wrinkled up her face in disgust. "I wish he were here right now."

Moni giggled, remembering they were in a girls' bathroom.

"Big talkers like him usually turn out to be wimpy, whiny little mama's boys in real life," Denise said.

"Cameron? I doubt it," Moni said.

Denise sighed. "It's just too bad he was

your first American. Just think how different things would have been if someone as nice as, say, Jennifer had come to stay with you."

"Or Nora," Moni said.

"Yeah. If you'd had someone nice, your whole family might have immigrated to America!" Denise said, switching to English. "Or is it emigrated? I always get those words mixed up."

Hearing English again reminded Moni of the mess she was in, and her eyes once again filled with tears.

"Oh, Moni, don't cry," Denise said, patting her shoulder. "People will understand about the phony background. I'll explain it to them. See, over here, how much money your family has just doesn't matter as much. And anyway, I've found that people are always a lot more forgiving than you think they're going to be . . . especially if whatever you've done hasn't really hurt them any."

"But what about the bake sale?" Moni wailed.

"That one's tougher," Denise said. She stared at the floor for a long minute. "But don't worry about that, either," she finally said. "I think I may have a solution."

Chapter 17

When Moni got out of Mrs. Bryant's car that evening carrying Mrs. Bryant's toaster oven, Nora and Jennifer ran out of Jennifer's house and hugged her, toaster oven and all.

"Please forgive me!" Moni said.

"We forgive you!" the girls said together.

"It was always *you* we liked, Moni," Nora said. "Not the shopping sprees in London or the international baking empire."

"And don't worry," Jennifer added. "Everything's going to turn out just fine. This way it'll be more fun, anyway. How much fun would it have been to just unload ready-made stuff off a truck?"

Moni smiled warmly at Jennifer. "It would have been much easier, at least. But thanks for being so nice about it."

"Thank Denise," Jen said. "This was all her idea."

They went inside to the kitchen, where Jeff tied an apron around each of them, even though they were wearing sweatshirts and bell-bottom jeans — and Moni could tell that Jen and Nora were wearing them as a special, private joke.

"How domestic," Nora snickered.

A minute later, Denise and her mother rang the doorbell. The girls were soon carrying in sack after sack of groceries from the Hendrixes' car.

"Mrs. Hendrix, I don't know how we'll ever be able to thank you for buying all of this," Jennifer said, unpacking flour, sugar, and a variety of spices in small bottles.

"It's quite all right, " Mrs. Hendrix said. "Just last week, Denise's father and I talked about making a donation to the animal shelter. This seems like a fine way to do that. At any rate, most of the donation will be yours, since you girls are doing all the work."

"Along with Jeff here," Denise said, coming through the kitchen door with two more toaster ovens. She introduced the Manns' housekeeper to her mother.

Within an hour after Mrs. Hendrix left, Jennifer and Nora were filling their first batch of éclair shells with custard, Moni and Denise were frosting their first dozen petit fours, and Jeff was pulling his first tray of cookies from the oven.

"Chocolate chip cookies?" Nora cried in her snootiest tone. "How veddy veddy bourgeois, my dear Jeff. How veddy common and ordinary."

"You think a teenage boy is going to spend his money on those?" Jeff boomed, pointing at the tiny petit four cakes. "He'd have to eat two dozen of them just to whet his appetite." Jeff took off his own voluminous apron and headed for the kitchen door with a big bowl of cookie batter. "Back in a few. I'm going to put a couple more batches in Debby's oven."

"I love him," Moni giggled when he left.

"Better not let Debby hear you say that," Jen teased.

Nora cleared her throat. "Speaking of love, Moni, there's one more mystery about you we haven't figured out."

"Yes?" Moni said.

Nora tried to keep her voice casual, her face straight. "Why do you like Jason better than the other guys?"

All three girls turned to look at Moni, heads cocked, eyes narrowed with curiosity.

Moni stared back at them as if they were

crazy. "Well, first of all, of course, because he is a — oh, how you say? — *rouquin?*"

Everyone looked at Denise. "*Rouquin?*" Denise repeated. "*Rouquin* . . . I just can't remember what that means."

Moni frowned, concentrating hard. "Oh . . . you know . . . he is a . . . red top?"

Nora laughed. "A redhead!" she cried. "She likes Jason because he is a redhead!" Denise and Jennifer laughed, too.

"Why is that so funny?" Moni demanded.

"It's just that . . . well, that's the one reason that never occurred to anybody, that's all," Nora said.

"But why not?" Moni asked. "Certainly it is true that redheads — as you call them — they are the most sought after, the most *désirable,* the most *populaire* boys in America."

"They are?" Jennifer asked, wide-eyed.

"Cameron, he had bright red hair," Moni continued, seeming not to have heard Jennifer, "and he had *six* girlfriends."

"Well, Moni, I think you're laboring under one last great misconception about Americans," Denise began, but Nora kicked her gently to shut her up. "Be diplomatic," Nora hissed.

"La–boring? Mis–con–ception?" Moni looked perplexed as she tried to pronounce these big English words that were new to her.

"Moni, let's just say your hypothesis about American redheads is an interesting one," Nora said, "and maybe it's correct in L.A. But in Jason's case . . . well, your hypothesis just doesn't hold water here in Cedar Groves."

But Moni had lost interest in the discussion — partly because she didn't understand the meaning of the slang expression "doesn't hold water." "Jason!" she said dreamily. "It is more than just the fact that he is a *rouquin* . . . he is also so sophisticated . . . so *romantique* . . . he writes like a philosopher in love."

The other girls turned back to their work and quietly gagged.

Meanwhile, several blocks away, the *rouquin* himself was finishing the display for his science project — WHAT IS THE OPTIMUM WHEEL SIZE FOR SKATEBOARD SPEED? — and worrying about Moni. She'd been out of school for days and then today, her first day back, she hadn't even glanced at him in biology. Nor had she come looking for him in the cafeteria at lunch.

He frowned as he glued the last of his test wheels — a two-and-a-quarter-incher — onto the display board. Well, it must have finally happened this time. Moni had somehow, somewhere, found out what Jason was really like. Maybe she had had second thoughts about those weird pictures of him.

Jason swallowed painfully. He was going to miss being a man women would die for. He was going to miss the looks of awe from the other guys; the new respect in the eyes of . . . well, at least a *couple* of girls. Jason swallowed again, and his throat felt raw. Though he hadn't been within ten feet of her in weeks, he wondered if he might have caught whatever Moni had.

Hey — wait — maybe that was it! Maybe Moni had just felt too *sick* today to think about love. After all, when she'd rushed out of biology, she'd looked on the verge of barfing!

"You're still in there, Anthony," he assured himself, idly smoothing down the cut-out letter "B" in his project title. And then, all of a sudden, he remembered something terrible. He had overheard Jennifer and Nora talking about some sort of all-girl bash Jennifer was having at her house tonight . . . and Jason distinctly remembered Nora mentioning Moni's name.

"Oh, no!" he groaned, falling across his bed in defeat. In his opinion, slumber parties were the worst enemies of the male species. On the Monday after one of those things, girls always came back to school smirking at the guys, full of disdain and new nicknames and private jokes. At this very minute, sick or not, Moni was probably listening to a million totally exaggerated Jason stories. He could just hear her: "Oh, that is so — how you say — *grossier*?" (Jason had looked *that* word up in his French/English dictionary.)

He rolled off his bed with a sigh and headed for his desk and his old friend, *The Greatest Poems of All Time*. As usual, he had no other choice. He had to do something to counteract the damage the slumber party was no doubt doing. In fact, he was going to have to slip whatever poem he chose into the Bryants' mailbox tomorrow, Saturday, so that Moni would have more than just the slumber party stories to think about when she thought about him this weekend.

None of the anonymous love poems grabbed him this time, but one that was written by a Percy Bysshe Shelley seemed perfect — it sounded nice but was pretty vague. Jason copied just the first stanza on notebook paper (the second stanza made a few references to kissing, which Jason considered unnecessary at this point):

Love's Philosophy

The fountains mingle with the river
And the rivers with the ocean,
The winds of heaven mix forever
With a sweet emotion;
Nothing in the world is single,
All things by a law divine
In another's being mingle —
Why not I with thine?

When he finished, he felt a little guilty about "borrowing" a poem that actually had a byline. But in the end, he decided that anyone who had a name like "Percy" and used words like "thine" was probably long dead and therefore wasn't going to mind helping out a fellow guy . . . a *desperate* fellow guy.

Jason signed the poem in the usual way, with the usual flourish. And then the *épouvantail rouquin* went to bed.

Chapter 18

Up until 5:03 P.M., the day of the Fifteenth Annual Cedar Groves Junior High Science Fair was one of the best of Jason's entire life. All afternoon, his project had attracted a crowd of admiring boys, though they were mostly sixth- and seventh-graders. All afternoon, many of them had waited patiently — sometimes even forming a *line* — to get Jason's expert opinion on skateboard matters. He felt brilliant, superior, *important.*

"Wow, do those ultra-rad wide trucks you've got on your board really work as well as the ads say they do?" one guy asked.

"It depends on the terrain," Jason said crisply.

"What hill did you test the wheels on?" another guy wanted to know. "How steep was it?"

"Can't you read?" Jason said haughtily. "It's all right there under 'methods.' "

It was at 5:03 that Jason saw Moni hurrying toward him through the crowded aisles of science projects, waving the poem he'd put in her mailbox that morning.

Oh, no. He'd assumed she wouldn't be there today because she hadn't done a science project. But he'd forgotten all about the bake sale.

Jason prepared to escape. There were a couple of sixth-graders pestering him with dumb questions, but who cared if they thought he was rude? "Gotta go," he muttered, interrupting one of them mid-sentence. He moved a few feet away from his project.

And then, disaster. Mr. Rochester, Jason's English teacher, suddenly blocked his path. "A great project, Jason," the teacher said. "And I need your advice. I'd like to buy a skateboard for my nephew for his birthday. But my primary consideration is safety, not speed, since he'll only be seven. What brands and styles would you recommend?"

Ditching a couple of sixth-graders was one thing. Ditching a teacher a week before report cards was unthinkable. Jason was stuck. Within seconds, Moni was beside him. She grabbed his arm in a viselike grip and smiled at Mr. Rochester as Jason muttered a couple of brand names.

"I would have come to see you earlier,

Jason, but I was too busy with the bake sale," she said.

"How is the bake sale going, Moni?" Mr. Rochester asked.

"*Fantastique*! In fact, everything is sold now . . . all the petit fours and croissants and éclairs." She giggled. "But the cookies went first." She drew one from the pocket of her pink blouse and handed it to Jason. "I saved one for you, though, Jason."

Mr. Rochester moved on to the next project.

"I wanted to tell you that your latest poem was *magnifique*, as usual," Moni said to Jason.

"Uh . . . thanks," Jason said, shoving the cookie into his mouth. It would provide — at least for a few minutes — a very good excuse for why he wasn't saying anything brilliant, witty, or sophisticated.

Moni, who was still holding onto Jason's arm with an iron grip, began to pull him away from his project. "I ask, why don't you walk me home? A walk in the twilight will be so *romantique*, no?"

"No!" Jason mumbled, desperately trying to swallow and clear his mouth of cookie as she pulled him toward the exit. "I can't leave!" he finally managed to say. "Um . . . we're required to stay at our projects and answer questions!"

"The fair and bake sale ended at five," Moni said, pulling him along.

"*Officially*. But Mr. Morris told us that we have to stay as long as there are people here," Jason lied.

Up on the auditorium stage, Mr. Morris had just stepped in front of the microphone. "Thanks for attending the Fifteenth Annual Cedar Groves Junior High Science Fair, folks," he said. "Unfortunately, because of school rules, now that it's five o'clock we're going to have to clear the auditorium immediately."

Mr. Morris, you traitor.

"But what about my science project?" Jason protested weakly to Moni as they went through the door. "We're not supposed to leave our projects here over the —"

"The school newspaper staff has requested that students leave their projects here over the weekend," Mr. Morris boomed over the mike. "They'd like to take pictures on Monday."

He was doomed. He was going to blow it, for sure.

Outside, the air was chill, but the sky to the west was a brilliant mixture of soft pinks and glaring oranges. Jason and Moni walked a block in total silence, her hand still gripping his arm. It was the first time

Moni had been so close to Jason, and she was surprised to find that he was much shorter than she had thought. And his arm —it was so *maigre*, so skinny. Had he not yet grown muscles?

"You are so quiet, Jason," she said.

He struggled for a minute but finally remembered something sophisticated: "My mind has been brimming with myriad deliberations of late." It was almost a direct quote from that first letter he'd written her. He hoped she wouldn't remember.

But she did, of course, having practically memorized every word he'd ever sent her. The look she threw him was both slightly surprised and curious.

"Isn't it a gorgeous sunset?" she asked after another half-block of silence.

Again, Jason racked his brain, this time in search of a French word. Finally . . . he got one! "Yes, it is *très beau*," he said, pronouncing it "tress bue."

She stopped, dropped his arm, and faced him with a puzzled expression. "What is tressbue? It is an English word that I do not know."

"But it's French," Jason said. "It means very beautiful."

Moni bit her lip for a long minute. "I think you mean *très beau*," she finally said, pronouncing it "tray bo."

Jason turned so red that his freckles

disappeared. Moni studied his face and was surprised to see that it was as smooth and hairless as her own. How many years would it be before he could grow a mustache as *splendide* as some of those she had seen in the high school?

"Do not be embarrassed," Moni said. "Everybody mispronounces foreign words at times. You should have heard me the first time I tried to say 'bumble bee.' Mrs. Bryant fell off her chair laughing."

"At least you're not laughing at me," Jason muttered.

"Because I have been in your position so many times myself."

Still, Jason was sure she was laughing inside. He had to get away from her. Another blunder like that and he'd blow it with Moni once and for all and for good.

He started to back away from her. "Look, Moni, I really have to go — "

In a flash, she reached out and captured his arm again.

" — I forgot that I promised to be home no later than five-fifteen," Jason said, trying to squirm out of her grasp as suavely as possible. How could such a tiny girl, he wondered, have a Hulk Hogan grip? It was as if her hand were a handcuff.

Moni felt a twinge of irritation. He was trying to run away from her. What a childish thing to do!

"See, my aunt . . . uh . . . Jane who we haven't seen in ten years is taking us out for dinner," Jason continued.

"Oh, Jason," Moni wailed, "I cannot, I *will not* go through another day without hearing some of your *magnifique* poetry . . . *in person*!"

Jason stifled a groan of dismay. "Here, give that to me," he said, nodding at her other hand, which clutched that morning's poem. "I'll read it to you."

She shook her head. "No. I want something you have not already sent to me. Just think of something as we stand here. Come up with a few beautiful lines just for me, and I will let you go, I promise."

If she hadn't been holding onto Jason, he might have keeled over in panic. What was he going to do? He fervently wished there would be a sudden cloudburst, or that a policeman would come along and arrest them for loitering, or even that a car would careen around the corner and jump the curb, forcing them to leap apart. *Anything* to distract her from this stupid idea of hers.

No such luck. There was not another soul in sight, not another sound to be heard.

"Come on, Jason. Your aunt Jane will be getting angry. Think of something quickly. Think of something *magnifique*."

Jason's tortured brain went to work

feverishly, snatching and rejecting words and phrases and syllables, trying to fit them together in rhymes. Finally, he came up with something he considered passable. "Okay, I have a poem for you," he said.

Moni nodded, her green eyes wide with anticipation.

Jason blurted it out:

"If I had the money
I'd like to give to you
A two-week trip
To Honolulu."

Moni's face fell ever so slightly, and she stared at him, silently running over the words of the poem in her mind. And then she laughed gently . . . and a little sadly. Because all of a sudden, she understood what had been bothering her since they had left the auditorium. All of a sudden, she realized that the difference between thirteen, as Jason was, and fourteen, her own age, was far, far greater than she had ever believed. All of a sudden, she saw that, regardless of the way Jason came off on paper in his poems and letters, in person, he was simply too young for her.

She released his arm, but her smile was warm and kind. "Jason, the real reason I asked you to walk home with me today was to tell you that . . . Jason, I like you so very much, but I am simply too uncomfortable with the difference in our ages to continue our relationship. I am sorry to be so petty . . . and I know it's not — how you say? — ah, yes, *liberated.* I know it is not liberated to be embarrassed about liking a younger man. Still, that is how I feel. And that is what I wanted to say."

Jason's mouth dropped open, and as her words sank in, he waited for his throat or stomach to hurt. Instead, to his surprise, he felt like a thousand balloons that had suddenly been released into the sky.

Moni gave him her distinctive little wave and began to walk away. "Good-bye, Jason."

"Add-i-ooh, Moni," Jason called after her.

"*Adieu,* Jason," Moni replied, pronouncing it "ad-you" and wondering if that was what he'd been trying to say.

Chapter 19

On Monday morning, Nora and Jennifer stood on the school's front steps, as usual, waiting for the bell to ring.

"Well, neither of us won a prize in the science fair, but the bake sale, at least, was a raging success," Nora said.

"And wasn't Moni a blast to work with?" Jennifer said. "I mean, both the night we did all the baking and then at the sale. She's just so cute and funny and sweet."

"I think we finally got to see the real Moni," Nora said. "And I'm going to miss her."

"Miss her? But she'll be here a few more months."

"Still, I don't think she'll be hanging out too much at the junior high anymore," Nora said.

"Why not?"

Discreetly, Nora pointed over Jennifer's

shoulder. Jen turned around. Both girls watched Moni walking hand in hand toward the high school with a guy who was smiling down into her eyes. He was tall and muscular. He also had bright red hair and a matching mustache.

Jennifer giggled. "Another *rouquin!* That's Jon Bremer."

Nora nodded, very impressed. "He's a *junior.*"

Tommy and Mitch came up beside the girls. They, too, were staring after the new couple.

Mitch whistled softly. "Red hair," he said. "It's the one hypothesis we never thought of."

"Neither did we," Nora told him.

Jason whizzed up on his skateboard and, jumping off, joined the crowd. He caught a glimpse of Moni and Jon before they disappeared through the high school doors.

"What happened, Jason?" Tommy jeered. "Did Moni Gorgeous finally catch up with you, get a close-up look at your face, and run away screaming?"

Jason tried to hide his surprise. So some of the guys suspected that he'd spent more time running from Moni than romancing her. He drew himself up to his full height. "You are implying that I used evasive tactics with Moni," he said haughtily, "and you are mistaken." He forced a frown.

"What broke Moni and I up was, unfortunately, a tragic misunderstanding."

But suddenly, that thousand-balloons feeling of relief flooded over Jason again. He no longer *had* to come up with phrases like "evasive tactics" and tragic misunderstanding." He no longer had to keep looking over his shoulder in fear of seeing bouncing black hair. He was free to once again hang out on the front steps before school. He was free of the Sony Walkman. He was free, free, *free* to be himself again!

Jason grinned at Jennifer while sticking out his tongue to provide a graphic presentation of the gum he had been chewing.

"Oh, gross!" Nora started to move away from him. But in further celebration of his new freedom, Jason stuck a foot out in front of Nora just long enough to throw her off-balance and send her books flying all over the steps.

"Grow up, Jason!" yelled Tracy, who had just arrived with Susan and Lucy. The girls helped Nora pick up her books.

"Problem: How can you get rid of Jason Anthony?" Jennifer asked the others.

"Hypothesis: Insult him," Lucy said.

"Method: Take off, pizza face!" Susan said to Jason.

He just gave her his disgusting, gum-on-tongue grin.

"Conclusion," Nora said with a sigh.

"Getting rid of Jason Anthony is — how you say? — *impossible!*"

What's an eighth-grader to do when a visiting grandmother starts making strict new rules to follow? Read Junior High #10, THE BIG DATE.